BEATRIX POTTER'S
LAKELAND

BEATRIX POTTER'S
LAKELAND

Hunter Davies

Photography by

Cressida Pemberton-Pigott

FREDERICK WARNE

FREDERICK WARNE

Published by the Penguin Group
27 Wrights Lane, London W8 5TZ, England
Viking Penguin Inc., 40 West 23rd Street, New York, New York 10010, USA
Penguin Books Australia Ltd, Ringwood, Victoria, Australia
Penguin Books Canada Ltd, 2801 John Street, Markham, Ontario, Canada L3R 1B4
Penguin Books (NZ) Ltd, 182–190 Wairau Road, Auckland 10, New Zealand

Penguin Books Ltd, Registered Offices: Harmondsworth, Middlesex, England

First published 1988
1 3 5 7 9 8 6 4 2

Text copyright © Hunter Davies, 1988
Rupert Potter's photographs copyright © Frederick Warne & Co., 1988
All colour photographs copyright © Cressida Pemberton-Pigott, 1988
The remaining photographs are reproduced by courtesy of the following:
p. 6 Joan Duke; p. 21 Rosalind Rawnsley; pp. 35, 124 National Trust;
p. 52 Winifred Boultbee; p. 66 John Heelis; p. 150 M. C. Fair;
p. 202 J. Brownlow; p. 224 Betty Hart

ISBN 0 7232 3520 1

Design by Mander Gooch Callow
Colour separation by Imago Publishing Limited
Photoset by Rowland Phototypesetting Ltd, Bury St Edmunds, Suffolk
Printed in Italy by L.E.G.O., Vincenza
A CIP catalogue record for this book is
available from the British Library

HALF TITLE PAGE: *Esthwaite Water, home of Mr Jeremy Fisher, which Beatrix Potter considered the most beautiful of all the lakes* TITLE PAGE: *Derwentwater and Lingholm Island* CONTENTS PAGE: *Penning the sheep at Patterdale Sheep-dog Trials*

Contents

Lakeland: An Introduction 7

Derwentwater 21

Hill Top 49

Sawrey and Hawkshead 63

Farming 83

Sheep 105

Lakeland Sports and Shows 133

Flowers, Fungi and Gardens 161

Tourism 181

Lasting Portraits 205

Lakeland: An Introduction

Beatrix Potter was an off-comer. So what's wrong with that? Lots of Lakeland lovers, people we will for ever associate with the Lake District, because they wrote or painted or generally raved about it, began as total strangers, come from another county and another culture. Coleridge and Southey were from the West Country. Ruskin was from London. De Quincey came from Manchester and Arthur Ransome came from Leeds, not too far away. Hugh Walpole came furthest, all the way from New Zealand. In more modern times the Blessed Wainwright, the sage of Kendal, is pure Lancashire, from Blackburn, and his accent has never changed. Chris Bonington, the seer of Caldbeck, is a Londoner, though in his case he has picked up a Northern accent on his travels. The exception amongst the all time greats in Lakeland enthusiasts is of course W. Wordsworth: a true Cumbrian, born and bred, lived and died (though clever clogs could say, ah ha, but the family did originally come from Yorkshire).

Mr Wordsworth is probably the wordsmith whose name comes most quickly to the mind when one thinks of Lakeland writers – which is only right and proper as befits a poet who was touched with genius – but it can be argued that Beatrix Potter is the most popular of them all. Her Lakeland home, Hill Top, is the single most visited literary house in the Lake District, despite its small size and the efforts of the National Trust to reduce the number of visitors. As for book sales, there is just no competition. Volumes of Wordsworth's collected poems trickle on quite nicely every year, selling around five thousand copies. With Ms Potter, a veritable flood, a torrent of those distinctive little books, swamps bookshops and souvenir shops round the civilised world. Beatrix Potter has been an industry, right from the time her first book appeared, *The Tale of Peter Rabbit*. In 1987, printings of that one title alone, still published by Frederick Warne, came to three hundred thousand copies.

She sells because she's loved, and she's loved because she's part of so many of our childhoods. She's also part of Lakeland. When the time came for her to give up writing and watercolouring, she devoted her life to working for the Lake District, but her words and watercolours still show the area to millions who will never be lucky enough to visit it. The Lakeland she knew lives on, give or take a few changes. The trannies have taken over from the 'gramophoning', the motorway has displaced the little local railways, but the landscape remains, the mountains and lakes, fells and dales. And we have her to thank that so much of it has been so perfectly preserved. What she got out of the Lakes she richly put back. We can look at Lakeland today through her eyes, seeing the activities and events which she enjoyed, the flora and fauna she captured in her work. We can chart the various stages of her love affair with the Lakes and understand today exactly

LEFT: Beatrix aged about ten, photographed by her father

what she saw and felt. It was a love affair, full of all sorts of passions; some of them rather potty, but then that is the way with off-comers. They so often see things more clearly than the natives, appreciate what the locals take for granted, become determined to save what they see disappearing. Even with Wordsworth, it was the experience of not being in Lakeland but stuck far away in a small town in Germany, which made him realise who he was, where he came from, and prompted him to begin *The Prelude*, the story of his life.

Beatrix Potter came to Lakeland from an urban background, a very different sort of life, and when she fell into the local ways, she did take quite a tumble, head over heels. Was it really necessary to wear those clogs? Did she have to dress like a farm yacker? And if you're going to take up farming, no one would really specialise in Herdwick sheep if they didn't have to, either then or today. But that's what converts do. It's not a matter of sense, but of sensitivity, soaking up all the new sensations, sinking deep into your adopted land.

It was not a totally foreign land for Beatrix, as she did have in her blood some very strong Northern connections. The family money came from Lancashire cotton and on both sides her folks were Lancashire folk. After all, until the recent county reorganisations, North Lancs included Furness and southern Lakeland, now swallowed up in Cumbria. And her grandfather, Edmund Potter, was MP for Carlisle, the county town of Cumbria. She could boast she was returning to her roots, though it all happened quite by chance.

RIGHT: Derwentwater and Catbells, photographed by Rupert Potter in September 1906

Beatrix Potter was born in London on 28 July 1866, at 2 Bolton Gardens, Kensington. (The house was destroyed by a German landmine in 1940.) Her father Rupert was a barrister, though he does not appear to have done a lot of barristering, devoting most of his time and energies to the Arts: visiting galleries and museums, collecting paintings, meeting his artist friends at their studios. He had done some gentle watercolouring himself, but his main creative urges went into the new and wonderful art of photography, at which he was quite expert and terribly enthusiastic. After a hard day giving himself to the Arts in some form, he would then relax in the evening at his club. His wife, Helen Leech, brought quite a bit of money to the marriage. She too was from a Unitarian, Lancashire cotton family. She devoted most of her energies to entertaining, leaving calling cards during the day at the homes of other Kensington ladies, and in the evening arranging splendid dinner parties. Their house was four storeys high, recently built, with an ample supply of servants. There was a cook, housekeeper, butler, coachman and groom, and when their first child, Beatrix, was born, a nurse was engaged. Around six years later, another child was born, Bertram. Like his big sister, he lived his life in the nursery on the top floor, hardly ever seeing his parents.

LEFT: *Grange and Borrowdale, Rupert Potter, September 1897. The Potters were staying nearby at Lingholm, Keswick, for their annual summer holiday.*

Mrs Potter was aloof and distant, as far as Beatrix was concerned, but Mr Potter did have more contact with his daughter. As she got older he took her to galleries and exhibitions and encouraged her when she started making little sketches, copying flowers and plants or her pets. She was also in demand to pose for his photographic sessions. You did have to pose in those days, arranging yourself nicely and then sitting absolutely still, but the results to this day are excellent. Mr Potter took his photographs as a gifted amateur, a dilettante even, but one who tried ever so hard. He once photographed Mr Gladstone for his friend Millais who used the photograph as a crib when painting Gladstone's portrait.

Mr Potter also had a circle of radical political friends, notably John Bright, a family friend from Lancashire, who often visited. He considered himself a Liberal, supported the right causes and interested himself in the social problems of the day, but he led a totally conventional life, as far as we can see. Despite knowing people like the pre-Raphaelite painters, he appears not to have had any bohemian characteristics, unlike some of his friends. (Millais, as a young artist, had gone off with Ruskin's wife.) He ran his home and brought up his two children in an utterly traditional way. Bertram, being a boy, was sent off to school when the time came. Beatrix stayed behind, under the care of a sequence of governesses. Her place was at home, doing nice

ABOVE LEFT AND RIGHT: Esthwaite Water, photographed by Rupert Potter in August 1896, when the family was staying at Lakefield (now Ees Wyke) in Sawrey. Beatrix's Journal *for that month records many excursions with her father to photograph the views.*

things, like painting watercolours, waiting for the next stage in her life, which was marriage to someone suitable when the time came. She accepted such a role, that of dutiful daughter, obedient to her Mama and a companion for her Papa should he require it.

It might seem surprising that with all the family interests and contacts in the art world, no one seriously encouraged Beatrix to be trained as an artist, or even to consider becoming one. She did meet Millais several times and went to his studio with her father. Girls were not considered suitable to be painters, however, though they might come into the art world through the side door as sisters, wives or mistresses of artists. Maybe no one thought she had any potential anyway, as she mainly copied things, neatly, carefully, but without showing any great originality or real talent. That all came much later. Nor had she been considered suitable to be educated, despite the fact that the first girls' schools had already opened in London (in the late 1840s). As for having a career, that was considered completely impossible. Girls of her class did not do such a thing. Working class women might have jobs, mainly in service, but in middle class families women did nothing at all. The Potters considered themselves upper middle, part of the professional classes. Nothing so posh as landed gentry or aristocracy, but a cut above business people, and certainly nothing so vulgar as trade. Florence Nightingale might have escaped from a similar affluent, upper middle class family and created a career, even a profession for herself, but that was most unusual and what struggles she had gone through.

Beatrix was caught firmly in the grip of her period, stuck with the conventions of her time and class. If only she had been born after the First World War, there would have been fewer barriers. But her parents were typical of the safe, solid late Victorian age, and she took the path that her mother had followed.

Could she be called deprived? Stuck alone up there in that top floor nursery, missing her brother away at school, and with no one her own age to play with or talk to, the picture of her life can be made to look rather sad. She was part of an affluent, stable family, though. No one was cruel to her. Mr Potter certainly considered himself a caring father, which he was, in the manner of his day. Beatrix did not feel hard done by, and why should she? Her life was pretty normal. There were lots of other girls sitting in top floor nurseries in London, looking out at their future, waiting and hoping, vaguely discontented but not knowing why.

RIGHT: Derwent Bay, Rupert Potter, August 1897

'It is all the same,' so she wrote, 'drawing, painting, modelling, the irresistible desire to copy any beautiful object which strikes the eye. Why cannot one be content to look at it? I cannot rest, I must draw, however poor the result, and when I have a bad time come over me, it is a stronger desire than ever, and settles on the queerest things, worse than queer sometimes. Last time, . . . I caught myself in the back yard making a careful and admiring copy of the swill bucket, and the laugh it gave me brought me round.' Now that would have been original and different: making paintings of such disgusting things, long before Francis Bacon had even been thought of.

Her sense of humour saved her that time, and in her letters as well as her *Journal*, her sharp, subtle wit is clearly seen. It might have surprised some visitors to the house, as she could appear so solemn and serious. When she was young, she looked a little Alice in Wonderland figure, quite pretty, but photographs show her becoming rather heavier and plainer as she got older.

As well as fussing over her pets, she could be clinical and scientific with animals, skinning a rabbit for example, boiling the bones, then reassembling the skeleton so that she could make a realistic drawing. She had in her nursery what amounted to a miniature zoo, with pet rabbits, mice, bats and other creatures all living with her.

The Potters might seem very indulgent in allowing such a situation. People of their class today would hardly condone such antics, refusing animals

LEFT: The shores of Derwentwater, photographed by Rupert Potter in September 1906. Beatrix had painted many similar scenes for The Tale of Squirrel Nutkin, *published three years before.*

in the bedroom for fear of dirt and germs, not to mention the stench. Certainly not, darling, that rabbit is going in the back garden at once, and no, you can't have the school hamster in bed with you. It has to be remembered however that the large staff at Bolton Gardens did the looking after, and Mr and Mrs Potter hardly ventured into the nursery quarters. Keeping animals was quite typical of the young Victorians. Elizabeth Barrett Browning, as a girl, had squirrels and rabbits in her room and later, as a young woman in Wimpole Street, she hatched a dove in her bedroom.

Beatrix's animals were one means of escape. She poured her love and her imagination into them, fascinated by what they did, and what she believed they thought, treating them as real people. At the age of fifteen she created another form of escape, a secret diary which she wrote in large chunks until she was thirty, using a code she had created. The code was not broken for over eighty years, but was eventually cracked in 1958 by Leslie Linder. Naturally all Beatrix Potter scholars were agog to find out what was in the *Journal*, to read about her secret life. It is a most interesting document, the daily life of a Victorian girl growing up, but there is nothing really dramatic in it. (Personally, I'd like to be given the secret diary of Rupert Potter, in the hope that he would tell the truth, or at least the club gossip, about his famous friends.)

My theory why she went to such trouble to write the diary in code is very simple. It was because she had no secrets. She was ashamed of the emptiness and boredom of her life and did not want any prying eyes, such as her mother's, to read about it. She just needed someone to talk to about herself, and as there was no one else in her life, she committed her

thoughts to her diary. In those pre-1900, pre-Freudian years, people did not talk out personal problems, even if they had any, or reveal their inner worries and fears, macabre thoughts or perverse longings. Nanny would soon deal with that sort of nonsense, otherwise it was a cold shower.

There was one real highlight to relieve the tedium every year, a delight which the whole family looked forward to, Beatrix and Bertram as well as their parents. This was the annual summer holiday which lasted for a whole three months, when they all went off, servants included, bags and baggages, decamping completely from London (which shows just how serious Mr Potter's barristering must have been). They were in the habit of taking a large country mansion, an estate with lots of land, somewhere in Scotland. For eleven years from 1871, they rented Dalguise House in Perthshire. Mr Potter and

their many visitors would shoot grouse, fish for salmon, stalk deer. Friends such as John Bright and William Gaskell, recently widowed (from Mrs Gaskell, the novelist) would join them for weeks at a time. During these long summer holidays, the two children were allowed a lot more freedom than in London, roaming the hills and burns, finding new animals, talking to the old ghillies and villagers.

In 1882, however, there was great gloom in the family when it was decided that they could not go to Dalguise any more. The old owner had died and the new people had put up the rent to what Mr Potter considered an exorbitant rate, £450 for the summer. So he refused to pay it. Mr Potter might have been well off, but there was good Lancashire commercial sense still running in his blood. (It is surprising therefore that he never bought a country home, as they all loved the countryside so much. Perhaps he

ABOVE: Looking towards Sawrey from Lakefield (now Ees Wyke), Rupert Potter, 1896
ABOVE LEFT: Hawkshead, Rupert Potter, August 1896. In her Journal, Beatrix records a visit to the town that month to see a travelling circus.

had worked out it was cheaper to rent, or he simply wanted to be free to try different places.)

On the rebound from Scotland, they decided to try the Lake District instead. Mr Potter found a suitably large and impressive house, rather Scottish in character, a mock castle on the shores of Lake Windermere called Wray Castle. As was the custom with so many of the large houses round the lake, it was built with Lancashire money. Wordsworth used to complain about the Liverpool and Man-

chester new rich building hideous holiday homes, though he himself ended up living in one for a while. (Perhaps that was why Mr Potter always rented, considering it vulgar to actually buy or build one's country pile.) A Dr Dawson from Liverpool had built Wray Castle in 1848, using his wife's inheritance from a gin fortune. She took one look at it when it was completed and refused to live there. Her husband eventually went bankrupt. The castle's architect drank himself to death. So much for a folly.

So in the summer of 1882, as Beatrix celebrated her sixteenth birthday, she came to the Lake District for the first time in her life; back to her roots in a sense, as that side of Windermere was still in Lancashire. A newcomer, then, if not totally an off-comer. One who was to make her name associated with Lakeland for ever.

Derwentwater

For the next twenty-one years, on and off, the Potters took their summer holidays in the Lake District, starting with Wray Castle in 1882. During that first summer, they explored all the little tarns hidden behind the western shores of Windermere. Beatrix and Bertram made a little expedition of their own to Hawkshead, some three miles away, getting lost and being chased by cows before they finally got there.

As usual, Mr Potter's grand friends came to visit them. William Gaskell came from his church in Manchester and John Bright came direct from the House of Commons, where he had resigned from the Cabinet over British intervention in Egypt.

The family also made a new friend, living almost next door: the vicar of Wray Church, which had been built at the same time as Wray Castle. He had just turned thirty, a young, handsome, muscular Christian called Hardwicke Rawnsley. A keen athlete and oarsman while at Oxford, he was also a would-be poet and writer. He had originally come from East Anglia, where his father had been a vicar, but had since become a great lover of all things Lake Districty, involving himself in local campaigns and movements to protect and preserve the country-side. His first great achievement was the formation of the Lake District Defence Society, which managed to number Tennyson, Browning, Ruskin and the Duke of Westminster amongst its members. Not bad for a local vicar, but then the Lake District had received national attention and affection since the days of Wordsworth and the Lake Poets. An analysis of the Defence Society's membership in the 1880s shows that of six hundred people, fewer than sixty, or ten per cent, were based in Cumbria.

LEFT: *Looking towards Catbells over Derwentwater*
BELOW: *Beatrix with Hardwicke Rawnsley and his son Noel, photographed by Rupert Potter at Lingholm*

At the time, Rawnsley was very active in a campaign to keep railways out of the Lake District, a battle which Wordsworth had also fought, and to stop Thirlmere being taken over by Manchester for its water supplies. This campaign received national attention in 1883, and Rawnsley appeared in a *Punch* cartoon, dressed as a shining knight. It turned out to be one of the very few campaigns he actually lost.

Another interest which brought him into contact with Rupert Potter concerned the Lake Poets. Mr Potter's latest hobby was collecting autographed letters by the Poets, and young Rev. Rawnsley was already an expert on this subject. He also took a great liking to Beatrix, praised her sketches and drawings, discussed the local flora and fauna with her, and explained the local geology and archaeology, all of which he knew a great deal about.

The Potters took Wray Castle for only one summer. The Castle is still there, now less of a folly and melding in well with the landscape, though still a surprising building to find in the middle of Lakeland. (Cumbria's big castles, the purpose-built ancient ones, tend to be on the fringes of the county.) You get the best view of it from across the other side of Lake Windermere. Today it is a naval college, for young men learning the more technical

RIGHT: *Daffodils at Lingholm*
BELOW: *Wray Castle, through the trees*

and electronic side of running communications at sea. You can walk round the grounds, down to the shore. Last time I was there, I met a man blowing tunes through a dandelion stalk, who then took me into a secret boat house where he was working on the rebuilding of three immaculate Victorian steam yachts, the sort the Potters took on their trips round the lake.

LEFT: *Derwentwater and St Herbert's Island, from Catbells*
BELOW: *Derwentwater, with Borrowdale in the distance*

The focus of their Lakeland holidays turned to Derwentwater, mainly to a house called Lingholm in which they stayed for six summers running, from 1885 to 1891. Later on they took the house next door, Fawe Park, for one year. Lingholm, now the home of Lord and Lady Rochdale, is known to all Lakeland lovers today for its gardens, particularly the rhododendrons. The gardens are open to the public.

Derwentwater is particularly loved for its light. Many photographers and painters find it the most stimulating of all the lakes to try to capture. It's an unusual shape as Lakeland lakes go, as the norm is long and thin with a few bends. Derwentwater is more chunky, fat and squat, one and a quarter miles wide, and surrounded by high mountains on all sides which keep the clouds moving, the light changing, the atmosphere different all the time. It is a great lake for boating, though not on the scale of Windermere, either for expensive yachts or the larger steamers. Because of its shape, it's very easy to get round. There have been regular services round the lake for many years, almost like a circular bus route, enabling visitors to pop off at one little pier, explore around, then pick up a later boat at one of the many other stops. There are four little islands in the middle, not served by the steamers but easy to get to in a rowing boat, canoe or dinghy.

Beatrix loved Derwentwater from the beginning. She explored Catbells, the gentle, roly poly fell almost behind Lingholm which has been adored by generations of families: so easy and satisfying to climb, admiring your progress and the lake below all the while. She went out to the little islands, watched the squirrels in the woods by the shore, saw the rabbits in the vegetable gardens of the big house. She made many sketches of the landscape around Derwentwater, filling little notebooks with her watercolours.

The move to Derwentwater did not mean they lost touch with Rev. Rawnsley. In 1883, after five years at Wray, he had been moved to Crosthwaite, just outside Keswick. (Crosthwaite Church is where Southey is buried, Poet Laureate before his friend Wordsworth. Southey's grave is still there, nicely restored by the grateful people of Brazil in 1961, for he recorded the first history of that country, without ever having visited it.) Rawnsley still discussed art and nature with Beatrix, encouraging her little drawings. In 1895, he also became secretary of the newly formed National Trust for Places of Historic Interest and Natural Beauty, an organisation he had created with two other worthies, Octavia Hill and Robert Hunter. The first Life Member was Rupert Potter. The Trust's first property for conservation in the Lake District was at Brandelhow, on the shores of Derwentwater.

Rawnsley eventually became Canon Rawnsley, an honorary Canon of Carlisle Cathedral, and the author of many books about the Lake District, as well as verses and memoirs. Along with his wife, he also set up a School of Industrial Arts in Keswick. Canon Rawnsley was not just a visionary, a talker and writer, he was a doer. No one has achieved more for the Lake District in the last two hundred years. (Yet there is no modern biography of him in any Lakeland bookshop.)

RIGHT: Water gleaming through the grasses, Derwentwater

After every idyllic Lakeland holiday came the return to London, where life went on much as before in the Potters' Kensington home. Bertram eventually went on to Oxford, though he was not to be particularly successful there, and there were signs that he had started to drink, not in moderation alas. (In her secret *Journal*, Beatrix described his alcoholism as '*it* getting hold again'.) She herself was still the dutiful daughter, attendant on her mother, pursuing her own hobbies. She began to study fungi, which she had simply painted at first, but now looked at more closely, under a microscope. She did have a few art lessons with an outside teacher, as opposed to her governess, but these did not last long. To fill in the days and keep her mind occupied, she took to memorising the plays of Shakespeare. In her *Journal* she described the excitement of her first ever visit down the Strand and along Whitehall. She was aged twenty at the time.

Pets were still Beatrix's greatest pleasure. There had always been a great variety of animals since the early days, from bats to lizards, frogs to mice, but now rabbits became her main concern. She had one particular favourite called Benjamin Bouncer, or Benjamin Bunny, followed by Peter Piper, also known as Peter Rabbit. They were not wild rabbits, caught on the Lakeland fens and carted back to Kensington, but had been bought from pet shops in London. Benjamin Bouncer used to go for walks with his owner around Kensington, kept on a leather strap for his own safety. She endlessly sketched and painted the rabbits and made them do their party tricks if young children came to the house.

LEFT: Derwentwater

People had made a fuss over Beatrix and her pets when she'd been a little girl. Now she was well into her twenties, fast becoming a spinster lady, with no means of employment, no gentlemen callers, and no income in her own right. She yearned to have some money of her own, especially as her mother grew more demanding and then for a time her father became seriously ill. 'It is something to have a little money to spend on books and to look forward to being independent, though forlorn,' she wrote in her diary. She herself had had rheumatic fever very badly in her late teens which had resulted in the loss of some hair. Many of the photographs from then on show her with a hat, and later a hair piece.

In 1890, aged twenty-four, she earned her first ever bit of money. She sold six designs for a greetings card, based on Benjamin Bouncer, to a firm called Hildesheimer and Faulkner. She received six pounds and was thrilled, but kept it a secret for a week before telling the rest of the family. 'My first act was to give Bounce (what an investment that rabbit has been in spite of the hutches) a cupful of hemp seeds, the consequence being that when I wanted to draw him next morning, he was partially intoxicated and wholly unmanageable.'

Her success with the greetings cards made Beatrix think there might even be a demand for a whole book of her little drawings of animals. She submitted her sketches and ideas to a number of publishers, including Frederick Warne, but they all turned her down. For the next ten years, she seems to have lost most of her hopes of being published, concentrating more on the study of natural history.

RIGHT: A fallen Scots pine, Derwentwater

ABOVE: A Scots pine by the shores of Derwentwater, at Brandelhow. Beatrix included an almost identical tree in The Tale of Squirrel Nutkin.

LEFT: Derwentwater

ABOVE: *Beatrix and Canon Rawnsley in 1912*
LEFT: *Buttercups in the Newlands Valley. Mrs Tiggy-winkle lived in the hills above.*

It was in 1900 that Canon Rawnsley came to her help. He was by now a children's author, having written a book of verse called *Rhymes for the Young* which had proved very popular. He encouraged Beatrix to write and illustrate her own children's book, instead of waiting for publishers to offer her their ideas. So she completed a little story, called *The Tale of Peter Rabbit and Mr. McGregor's Garden*, by H. B. Potter. (Helen, after her mother, was Beatrix's first given name.) The idea was based on a letter she had written seven years previously from Scotland, to a little boy who was ill, son of her former governess, all about four little rabbits called Flopsy, Mopsy, Cottontail and Peter. She wrote the tale out neatly in a new exercise book, with all the illustrations except one in black and white (pen and ink) to keep the costs down.

Together, she and Canon Rawnsley drew up a list of likely publishers. The book went to six, and they all turned it down. (So much for Canon Rawnsley's expert advice on the London publishing scene.) So, still egged on by the good Canon, Beatrix decided to go it alone, using her own money. She found a printer and in December 1901, she privately published two hundred and fifty copies, priced one shilling and twopence each. Half of them were given away, as Christmas presents for friends. But they all went, and Beatrix ordered another two hundred copies to be printed.

Canon Rawnsley meanwhile was still determined to find her a proper, commercial publisher. He even decided to rewrite *Peter Rabbit* in his own verse, imagining that would do the trick. By now, Warne were much keener on the book, but they preferred Beatrix's own text and insisted that all the illustrations must be in colour. After agreeing this, and following lengthy discussions on the possible ways of printing, and on financial and copyright details (which Beatrix was very interested in), the contract was signed.

The Warne edition of *The Tale of Peter Rabbit*, Beatrix Potter's first public venture as an author, came out on 2 October 1902. The first printing was for six thousand copies, and all of them were sold out before publication. She was by now thirty-six. All those years looking for something she could do, and now her own little amusement had produced some work for her, a real income at last, and most surprisingly of all, an eager public. This audience greeted her first book at once with great enthusiasm, an enthusiasm that has never since died down.

Even before Warne had brought out *Peter Rabbit*,

Beatrix was ready with a second book, *The Tailor of Gloucester*, which she again had printed privately so she could include all the nursery rhymes in it that she feared Warne would want to cut. It appeared three months after *Peter Rabbit*.

The following year, Warne brought out two of her books for Christmas 1903, their shortened version of *The Tailor of Gloucester*, and a brand new story, *The Tale of Squirrel Nutkin*. 'I think my sympathies are still with the poor tailor,' so Beatrix wrote, 'but I can still believe the other would be more likely to appeal to people who are accustomed to a more cheerful Christmas than I am.' A rather pathetic note, not tinged with her usual oblique wit or self-awareness.

Squirrel Nutkin, her third book, was the first of what we now call the Lakeland books, a whole string of *Tales* based on places and things she had seen during her summer holidays. If you look at the books carefully, you can even recognise the background views, picking out Catbells, or Derwentwater, or the Newlands valley. Squirrel Nutkin is clearly paddling across Derwentwater to St Herbert's Island, for example. *The Tale of Benjamin Bunny*, which came out the next year, 1904, was set in the grounds of Fawe Park. Then came *The Tale of Mrs. Tiggy-Winkle* in 1905, another story set round Derwentwater which Beatrix had begun to think up at Lingholm in 1901. Lucie of Little-town who appears in the tale was based on a real Lucie: Lucie Carr, the daughter of the Vicar of Newlands, who was one of the Potters' many Lakeland friends.

During the summer of 1903, while staying at Fawe Park, Beatrix had completed a little sketch book, filling it with local scenes and views which she later used in these books.

ABOVE: St Herbert's Island, seen from the shores of Derwentwater
RIGHT: Woods fringing the Derwentwater shoreline

ABOVE: *Fawe Park, seen from the kitchen garden*

ABOVE: *Derwentwater, from the kitchen garden at Fawe Park*

BELOW AND RIGHT: Snow scenes in the Newlands Valley

LEFT: *Low Snab Farm, in the Newlands Valley. Beatrix wrote in a letter to her cousin, Caroline Hutton, 'Our pretty old whitewashed farmhouses in the sheltered valleys are a feature of the district.'*

FAR LEFT: *The Newlands Valley, looking towards Dalehead, the very view painted by Beatrix Potter for* The Tale of Mrs. Tiggy-Winkle.

BELOW: *Newlands Church. The Potters became friendly with the then vicar of Newlands while staying at Lingholm, and Beatrix put his daughter Lucie in* The Tale of Mrs. Tiggy-Winkle *as Lucie of Little-town.*

Beatrix bought her sketch book in Keswick, as is clear from the shop keeper's name – H. Slade Wilson, Bookseller, Stationer and Printer, Market Square, Keswick. Apart from all the Derwentwater views, there are some scenes in the book of Keswick itself, round the Moot Hall where all the stall holders were setting up for market day, and Beatrix has drawn a little girl who looks very much like the eventual Lucie in her book. It is unusual in her work to see any adult figures or even children, apart from Lucie. Beatrix was not so good at humans, and usually avoided painting them. In real life, she found dealing with people not much easier, at least not most gentlemen, with one exception.

The animals in Beatrix's books are also drawn from life, though rarely on location. She used her own pets, making them model for her in London, dressing them in the clothes she wanted them to wear. Mrs Tiggy-winkle was her own pet hedgehog, which she took with her almost everywhere, safe in a cardboard box. 'Mrs Tiggy as a model is so comical, but if she is propped up on end for more than half an hour, she begins to yawn pathetically.'

The summer of 1903 was the last for Beatrix on Derwentwater. Her parents, with whom she still had her holidays, decided to move to another lake. They always insisted on being near water. This time they took a house called Lakefield (now known as Ees-Wyke) in Near Sawrey, beside Esthwaite Water. Derwentwater had served them well, as had Canon Rawnsley, little Lucie, Benjamin Bunny, Mrs Tiggy and a whole host of red squirrels.

LEFT: The Moot Hall, Keswick, on market day
BELOW: Water cascading down Catbells, where Mrs Tiggy-winkle did her washing

RIGHT AND BELOW: Skating on Derwentwater

ABOVE: *The Keswick landing stage, Derwentwater*
LEFT: *Derwentwater*

Hill Top

Beatrix Potter's first purchase in Lakeland was a field in Near Sawrey in 1903, a minor stake in the countryside she had grown to love. Owning land in the Lakes is an ambition which millions have had over the years, and many have fulfilled. This particular plot was very near Lakefield, where the Potters spent their summer holidays, which was how Beatrix had come to hear about it. She explained it away to her father as an investment, a little piece of speculation. Her parents, naturally, did not want to consider for one moment that their unmarried daughter of thirty-seven might be harbouring thoughts of moving away from her family home and duties. Perish the very thought.

But life was changing for Beatrix, becoming exciting and active and, surprisingly, rather lucrative. By the end of 1903 there were fifty thousand copies of *Peter Rabbit* in print, and the *Tales* which followed were all doing well. She now had a bit of income of her own and could indulge herself, beginning at last to believe that she might even become moderately independent, at least from a financial point of view.

She involved herself in all aspects of the production of her little books, designing the end papers, thinking up the covers and even beginning to consider some merchandising possibilities. She had already seen pirate firms stealing her characters and using them on cheap shoddy goods, a practice we tend to think is a modern one, but the world of children's books and children's toys at the turn of the century was very competitive. All the same, it is

ABOVE: *Hill Top porch and front door, much as they were in Beatrix Potter's day*
LEFT: *The path leading up to Hill Top. In* The Tale of Tom Kitten, *Mrs Tabitha Twitchit led Tom, Mittens and Moppet up this very path to wash them and dress them inside the house.*

amazing, considering her background and her non-existent knowledge of business, that on 28 December 1903 she registered at the Patent Office in London a Peter Rabbit Doll. She cut out the calico patterns herself, devised the whiskers, and wrote to her publisher that she had high hopes Harrods would take it. She then invented a Peter Rabbit board game, patented that, and started on designs for Peter Rabbit and Benjamin Bunny wallpaper. She couldn't decide who to sell the rights to, either Sandersons who had offered ten pounds, or Liberty who might offer more. (We think that such merchandising began with Walt Disney and Mickey Mouse.)

By suddenly becoming a smart business woman, and a more than normally concerned author,

Beatrix was having a lot more dealings with her publisher, Frederick Warne and Sons. The one who looked after her was Norman Warne, youngest son of the firm's founder. She told him her ideas and he assiduously kept her in touch with developments, making sure every proof reached her and she knew of every decision. Norman wrote to her almost every day, either to Bolton Gardens or to the Lake District when she was on holiday. He was un-married and lived with his widowed mother and unmarried sister in the family house in Bedford Square, London. Norman invited Beatrix to his home, with a chaperone of course, and she became close friends with his sister, Millie.

Beatrix was working on an idea for a new book about two naughty mice, using, as ever, her own

LEFT AND BELOW: The dolls' house which is displayed at Hill Top. Although not the original one made by Norman Warne, it does contain some of the dolls' things that appear in The Tale of Two Bad Mice. *Hunca Munca steals the birdcage shown in the photograph below, for example, though it is too big to fit into the mousehole.*

pet mice as models. They needed a new cage, so she asked Norman if he would oblige, as she had discovered that he was a jolly good amateur carpenter and had recently made a dolls' house for his own niece. Beatrix planned to incorporate the dolls' house in the book as well, getting the bad mice to raid it. Norman was pleased to accept the assignment, and they discussed how one side of the new cage was to be of glass, so Beatrix could draw the mice as they scurried back and forth. Through these

ABOVE: Norman Warne
RIGHT: Chickens around the door at Hill Top

pleasant, ever so harmless, ever so touching discussions, a close friendship grew up. Could it, dare one imagine, turn into a romance? Hmm. Back home, in the Potter Mansion, they certainly began to think such might be the case, and were not best pleased at the prospect. The Warnes were definitely Trade. Not a suitable match for the Potters' dear and only daughter.

The Tale of Two Bad Mice came out at the end of 1904, yet another 'Potter for Christmas' (the new selling slogan in all the best London shops) and 30,000 copies were printed. Next year Beatrix began work on the story she had started to think up at Lingholm, *The Tale of Mrs. Tiggy-Winkle.*

There were two very happy events in the summer of 1905. Firstly, Norman proposed. He did it by letter, as after all he and Beatrix had still not been alone in each other's company. She was thrilled and accepted at once, without properly realising what her parents' reaction might be. They were most upset, considering she had been disloyal. She was admittedly now thirty-nine, rather old to be bossed around, but she was their only daughter and now the only child they could rely on, as Bertram had gone off to farm in Scotland. After some emotional discussions, it was decided that Beatrix could become engaged, but on two conditions. No public announcement would be made and no one outside the immediate two families would be informed. But she could wear Norman's ring, which was something.

The other excitement was the purchase of a real Lakeland property, not just a field, but a little farm in Sawrey called Hill Top. It was a small farm with a working farmer and his wife, whom Beatrix proposed to let stay on as sitting tenants. Once again

she announced it as an investment, putting her money into something she happened to love. She was not contemplating moving up to Hill Top, or even having her holidays there, as of course she would still take those with her ageing parents.

At the beginning of August 1905, Norman Warne fell ill. He had never been particularly strong, but no one imagined this illness would be so serious. He died of pernicious anaemia within three weeks, on 25 August 1905, at the family home in Bedford Square. Beatrix was devastated. She visited his grave in Highgate Cemetery, stayed with the Warnes for a while at their home, but could not face going back straight away to her parents' house in Kensington. She fled to the Lake District for a

while, ostensibly to see how the new farm was getting on, and to discuss the stock with the tenant farmer, Mr Cannon. Just as earlier she had thrown herself into her secret diary to escape her teenage anxieties, she now filled her life with sheep and pigs and new barns. It was a form of therapy, to take her mind off the tragedy of Norman's death, her fiancé of just a few months. He had been only thirty-seven.

For the next eight years, Beatrix devoted all her energy to two occupations: producing children's books every year, supervising their presentation and merchandising under the direction of Harold Warne, Norman's brother; and at the same time rushing up and down to the Lake District whenever

ABOVE LEFT AND RIGHT: Hill Top is still a working farm, run today by Geoff Storey, son of Tom, Beatrix Potter's former shepherd and farm manager

she could manage it, to look after her property. Her home was still in Kensington, and most years she managed only one month on her own in Lakeland. Her parents resented her new interest in farming, but they still took annual summer hols in Lakeland, which gave Beatrix more time in Sawrey. She was determined not to alter Hill Top but to leave the inside as it was, with no modern additions which might ruin the look or the feel of it. She did have a new wing built, however, to enable her to have some space apart from the Cannons.

She hired the workmen and tried if possible to supervise progress. 'I had rather a row with the plumber,' she wrote in a letter, 'or perhaps I ought to say I lost my temper! The men have been very

ABOVE: The parlour at Hill Top, dominated by the large fireplace which Beatrix herself had installed
RIGHT: The wall-cupboard in the parlour at Hill Top

go through the back kitchen ceiling . . . the joiner and plasterer were much alarmed and hauled me out. I was very much amused.'

She even appeared amused by the fact that the house had many uninvited visitors. 'The rats have come back in force; two big ones were trapped in the shed here, besides turning out a nest of eight baby rats in the cucumber frame. Mrs Cannon has seen a rat sitting up eating its dinner under the kitchen table in the middle of the afternoon. We are putting zinc on the bottom of the doors – and a cement skirting will puzzle them. . . . It is indeed a funny old house and it would amuse children very much.'

Eventually, in 1909, she bought another farm almost opposite, Castle Farm. This then became her main Lakeland base when she could get away, with Hill Top kept almost as a period piece. It was a working farm, but a most unusual one, where time stood still and the old ways continued.

The locals were rather amused and indulgent towards this funny little London woman coming into their village, who obviously had quite a bit of money to spend. She was well aware of what they thought of her, coming in as an 'off-comer', a total outsider to farming life. 'My purchase seems to be regarded as a huge joke,' she wrote. 'I have been going over my hill with a tape measure.'

Ah, the pride of possession. I remember buying a cottage and some fields at Caldbeck, and a beck that went with them, getting down on my hands and knees to see if the acreage agreed with the estate agent's claim. When I stood up, my back sore, I decided the beck was really rather handsome and I'd call it a trout stream from now on, even though it was narrow enough to step across.

good so far; if he won't take orders from a lady, I may pack him off and get one from Kendal.' On another occasion, she nearly did herself a nasty injury. 'The first thing I did when I arrived was to

ABOVE: *The kitchen hearth, the heart of Hill Top house. Horse brasses hang over the fireplace, and Doulton jugs and mugs flank a Staffordshire bust of John Wesley on the mantelpiece. A traditional rag rug lies in front of the grate, and Beatrix's clogs stand beside the spinning wheel.* Tom Kitten *climbs up this very chimney in* The Tale of Samuel Whiskers, *though the range shown in the book was removed in Beatrix Potter's time to make way for the grate and fireback.*

LEFT: *Looking up the stairs from the kitchen. Mrs Tabitha Twitchit stood on this landing and 'mewed dreadfully' when looking for her son Thomas in* The Tale of Samuel Whiskers.

The frequent visits to Hill Top over the next few years resulted in Beatrix's most productive period as an author and artist. She drew inspiration from Hill Top and the surrounding countryside and at least seven of her books are set in or around the farm. Tom Kitten's tale takes place in the house and garden at Hill Top, and Samuel Whiskers lived there too. Jemima Puddle-duck quacked around the farmyard and the little hills nearby while *The Tale of Ginger and Pickles* is set in the village shop. Mr. Tod also lived in the hills around Sawrey; Pigling Bland and Alexander set off to market from the Hill Top yard, and the farm also appears, together with other views of Sawrey, as a background for *The Tale of The Pie and The Patty-Pan.* You can still recognise these scenes today, as well as views in the books of other buildings in Sawrey, such as the Tower Bank Arms. From Hill Top farmhouse, Beatrix took details of the furniture and fittings, the fireplace and stairs to reproduce in her paintings.

In a sense, Hill Top became a 'model' farmhouse, deliberately arranged and preserved by Beatrix for several uses – not just to live in and love, but to be used as raw material for her drawings and water-colours. She had done the same with her animals, turning them from pets into models. This may sound cold-hearted and calculated, as if she had planned out each stage, but of course she had not. It all just happened. She was not to know that the public would be so wildly enthusiastic for her little drawings and stories. But once it had happened, she worked hard to maintain her own standards and keep Warne happy, with at least one new book every year until 1913.

Today, Hill Top is as it was, which was Beatrix's aim from the very beginning, though she did not imagine it would become a museum, a perfect example of a seventeenth-century Lakeland farm-house. Of course, it is not just the vernacular architecture which millions from around the world have come to ogle. They come to steep themselves in Potterdom, to breathe in the atmosphere, recog-nise the scenes and recall the incidents which took place there, if only in the owner's imagination. The entrance hall still has the same stone flags which appear in several of her books, typical of Lakeland farmhouses, as is the rag rug in front of the marvel-lous fireplace. The warming pan beside it, which was meant to hold hot water rather than coals, belonged originally to Beatrix's Lancashire grand-mother. Look out for Beatrix's clogs as well and

ABOVE: Pace eggs decorated by Beatrix Potter for the Sawrey children to use in their races at Easter
RIGHT, ABOVE: The kitchen dresser which appears in The Tale of Samuel Whiskers
RIGHT, BELOW: The bedroom Beatrix used when she visited Hill Top after her marriage. Her bible stands on the bedside table.

notice how small her feet were: size four. The furniture and paintings are those she collected, matching the style and flavour of the house. Up-stairs in her bedroom are some nineteenth-century French dolls which are said to have been the models for Jane and Lucinda in *The Tale of Two Bad Mice*. The dolls' house, in the so-called Treasure Room, is not the very one from that book, but contains the dolls' house food that Hunca Munca and Tom Thumb tried to eat. In the sitting room are various photographs of Beatrix with her father and brother.

When you visit Hill Top, the main object of pilgrimage for all Potter lovers, you are visiting a place of worship, where the first worshipper was Beatrix Potter herself.

Sawrey and Hawkshead

Near Sawrey and Far Sawrey are two little villages, no more than hamlets really, which straddle the road from the Windermere ferry. Millions of tourists over the years have seen them as they come up the hill from the lakeside. Most people are in cars these days, as the ferry takes motors, if not very many at a time. You come to Far Sawrey first, which must confuse some folks, though it is hard anyway for outsiders to tell where Far ends and Near begins. Beatrix Potter lived at the second hamlet, Near Sawrey, the one with the Tower Bank Arms. The distinction between the two villages was not to denote distance from the lake but to tell the world which was the closer to the centre of civilisation, as people on the western shores of Windermere have always known it. Hawkshead, in other words, the very model of a prim and proper, right and regular, square and handsome little market town.

You might wonder why they bother to differentiate, when Far Sawrey is less than two miles away from the town, and there's only half a mile or so between the two little settlements. It's not quite on the scale of the Far East as opposed to the Near East. But in Lakeland, you see, everything is on a small scale. It is God's miniature kingdom, with all the wonders and beauties of Nature decanted into a pocket-handkerchief of landscape. Perhaps that was what attracted Beatrix Potter. She is a miniaturist, contracting her art and her life into those tiny, immaculate pages.

Hawkshead always seems bigger than it is, with its narrow streets, intercommunicating passages, little cobbled yards, hidden alleyways, fine squares, pretty houses, inviting pubs and quite a few imposing, not to say splendid, buildings. It feels affluent and solid, with none of the tatty overtones that so easily diminish Bowness and Windermere at the height of the season. All the same, it is a tourist town, with the twee tea shops, the ancient pubs and the gift shops, all laid out for trippers. Thanks to that car park on the outskirts, an eye sore though it is when you first approach the town, Hawkshead however has remained traffic-free, so you can wander at will, admiring the architecture, trying to pretend that the other rubber-necks doing exactly the same don't really exist.

It has a resident population of just six hundred people, but they manage to keep up the heart and atmosphere of a real community, especially in the winter when the hordes have gone. In the old days, right back to Norman times, it was famous and affluent as a wool town, and even when this industry faded, Hawkshead remained vital as a market town. Its Grammar School can still be seen and visited today. Though just a little one, it sent scholars to the best universities. One of them was Wordsworth. He made that trip to school at Hawkshead, up the hill from the ferry and through the Sawreys, every term when he came from Penrith. The church still dominates one end of the town, 'snow white on a hill', as Wordsworth called it, 'like a throned lady.' It's not whitewashed any longer, but still as majestic.

RIGHT: The clean white houses of Hawkshead

ABOVE: Hawkshead Grammar School
*RIGHT: Beatrix and William Heelis on their wedding day, 14
October 1913*
*FAR RIGHT: Ann Tyson's cottage in Hawkshead: William
Wordsworth once lodged with her when he was at school*

Hawkshead proved a perfect little town for Beatrix to potter around, get her supplies, materials for her farm and cottage, or meet experts to help her. She used a local firm of solicitors, W. H. Heelis and Son, for her property purchases, which were now becoming quite regular, as she built a stake in and around Sawrey. She began to rely on William Heelis, youngest son of the firm's founder, to look after her local business and tell her what was coming on the market. He had gone to a local public school, Sedbergh, favoured by the county's professional people. (It was then in Yorkshire, now is part of Cumbria.) He was in partnership with his cousin, also called William Heelis. In the firm, one was called Appleby Willie and the other was Hawkshead Willie, just to make the difference clear. Hawkshead Willie, who became Beatrix's adviser, was tall and quite handsome, in a craggy, countrified sort of way. Locals said he looked a bit like Wordsworth. They have long memories, country folk, when you think that Daddy Wordsworth had died nearly sixty years before William and Beatrix met.

ABOVE: Ees Wyke, Sawrey, where the Potters stayed for several of their annual summer holidays (the house was then called Lakefield)
LEFT: Looking out over the countryside from Ees Wyke

William Heelis proposed to Beatrix towards the end of 1912. He was in his early forties, perfectly eligible, a good solid member of the community. But would a country lawyer be considered more suitable as a husband than a London publisher, or did law still smack of the dreaded word, 'trade'? The Potter parents were again not pleased, and this time there were added complications. Rupert, now eighty, was in very poor health. His wife, seven years younger, was not very robust either. Who would look after her if he went? Their only daughter of course. It was her duty to stay with them. (This is the trap that spinster daughters have fallen into for centuries. Even today, it still happens.) But Beatrix had at least made some sort of break, by buying her Lakeland property and turning all her thoughts towards it. Without Hill Top and Castle

Cottage (the house attached to Castle Farm), she might well have been caught at home in Kensington for ever.

The emotional blackmail which the Potters exerted on their family crumbled when Bertram, their only son, made a surprise announcement. He had been married for seven years, not working alone on his farm in the Scottish Borders as his parents had believed. He had kept his marriage a secret, knowing what their reaction would be. He was also still drinking heavily, but they did not know that either, and doing more painting and pottering around than actual farming. He had married a girl called Mary, daughter of a Hawick publican. Mary had at one time worked as a maid. This shocking revelation, along with Beatrix's obvious determination to get married, made the Potters finally consent. A

ABOVE: The view towards Esthwaite Water from Sawrey
ABOVE LEFT: Sawrey in the snow. Beatrix was fascinated by the winter countryside, and painted many snowy scenes of Sawrey and Hill Top.

lawyer was at least higher on the social ladder than a serving maid.

Beatrix Potter and William Heelis were married in Kensington, London, on 14 October 1913. They went back to the Lake District afterwards, hoping to move into Castle Cottage, though it was not quite ready. Just two weeks after they arrived, Beatrix was called back to London to help her mother. Rupert was ill and Mrs Potter was struggling with the task of interviewing and hiring a new parlourmaid. The next year, Rupert's condition got worse, and Beatrix was up and down on the train to London to help nurse him. Rupert died in May 1914. Beatrix brought her mother up to Sawrey and began looking for a local home for her, where she might live in the style to which she was determined to remain accustomed.

LEFT: *Castle Cottage, in which Beatrix and William Heelis lived after they were married*

BELOW: *Hill Top, seen from the little hills above the farm. Many of the characters from Beatrix Potter's* Tales *lived among these hills.*

ABOVE: *A back garden in Sawrey*
RIGHT: *Moss Eccles Tarn, where Beatrix and Willie often
rowed on a summer's evening, she to sketch and he to fish*

The marriage, therefore, began in some unsettled times. Beatrix herself had been ill the winter before. Then there were all the family troubles. Not to mention of course World War One, beginning somewhere out there. It might have seemed a bit remote at first in Hawkshead, but young men were being called up all the time, and eventually older men as well. Willie got his call-up papers, but this was towards the end of the war and he was not needed. Bertram volunteered, but his health excluded him. He died in July 1918, suffering a cerebral haemorrhage while working in his garden. He was forty-six.

Beatrix's latest little book, *The Tale of Pigling Bland*, came out the same month as her marriage. It was the last of the so-called Sawrey books, in which she used her own pigs from Hill Top Farm as models. This was one of the stories Graham Greene raved about in his essay devoted to her work, published in 1934. He praised her writing skill, her detachment and realism. Other later analysts have

pointed out that in this book, the first female pig in literature appears, Pig-wig.

'Inquisitive, demanding to be amused, fond of confectionary, and admirably un-selfconscious,' so Graham Greene described Miss Potter's feminine pig. (Doesn't that make her sound very like a later female pig, Miss Piggy from the Muppets?)

On the whole, Beatrix Potter has escaped the worst excesses of academic enthusiasm, post-Freudian interpretations and structuralist analysis. She herself gave short shrift to anyone propounding fancy intellectual explanations for her work. In that same essay, Graham Greene suggested that at some time around 1909 she had suffered an emotional ordeal, which explains the 'dark period of Miss Potter's art', as seen in *The Tale of Mr. Tod*. Beatrix Potter thought about it and told a friend yes, she did have a touch of flu during the writing of *Mr. Tod*.

Once she settled down to married life at Castle Cottage, where she was to live for the rest of her days, her writing life, her period as 'Beatrix Potter',

ABOVE: *The post office in Sawrey*
LEFT: *Buckle Yeat, used as Duchess's house in* The Tale of
The Pie and The Patty-Pan

was as good as over. The next of the little books did not appear for five years – *The Tale of Johnny Town-Mouse*, published in 1918. The town is Hawkshead, as you can tell from one of the paintings, while the gardens of Sawrey serve as the country.

Beatrix's creative period in effect lasted only thirteen years, from 1900 until her marriage, and this is when the bulk of her twenty-three little books appeared, though one or two dribbled out later on. She came to writing late, in her mid-thirties, as an escape and refuge from a stifling, isolated family life. Then, when she married at the age of forty-seven, she as good as gave it all up, no longer seeing herself as Beatrix Potter, children's writer, but Mrs Heelis, wife and farmer.

Was it happiness that made her retire? Had her books been a substitute for a happily married personal life? She herself said her eyes were too tired and she was not up to all that finicky, detailed work any more. She had also run out of good new ideas, judging by the later books, which are rather thin.

She was reworking old themes or unused material, whenever her publisher insisted that the public was desperate for a new Potter. Disliking all the fuss of being a Famous Writer, she had been determined to avoid all that and would not miss it. She'd finally succeeded in becoming what she decided she had always wanted to be, a Lakeland farmer. That was more important to her. She was now about to begin the next stage in her life, one which was to last for another thirty years.

RIGHT: A filing room at the Heelis offices before it was cleared to accommodate the new gallery
BELOW: The interior of William Heelis's office, just as it was when he was working there

In Hawkshead, Beatrix was already known simply as Mrs Heelis, wife of Hawkshead Willie the solicitor, which was what she preferred. She was a familiar figure in the town, popping into her husband's office, though she spent most of the time on her own concerns, back on the farm.

The office of Heelis the solicitors is still there, a delightfully old-fashioned building, left until recently much as it always was, with its Edwardian overtones and fading files and ledgers and desks. Recently, it has been cleaned up and houses the marvellous collection of Beatrix Potter's original watercolour book pictures, the ones which for many years were on show at Hill Top. The National Trust, sponsored by Frederick Warne, has done a good job and the place will prove another shrine for all Potter fans, perhaps taking some of the strain away from Hill Top. It's apt that the paintings should have come home to Hawkshead as their final resting place, back to Beatrix's neat little, stout little local town.

RIGHT: Formerly the Heelis offices, this building in Hawkshead now houses the exhibition of Beatrix Potter's watercolour book illustrations

Farming

Beatrix Potter, or Heelis as she preferred, was becoming increasingly absorbed by her life as a country farmer, and began to find it more and more difficult to spare the time for painting and writing her books. By 1920 she had become so exasperated with Warne's continual demands for new stories (for she was their most successful author and mainstay of the business) that she wrote, 'You do not realise that I have become more, rather than less obstinate as I grow older; and that you have no lever to make use of me; beyond sympathy with you and the old firm, nothing else would induce me to go on at all. I have never cared tuppence either for popularity or for the modern child; they are pampered and spoilt with too many toys and books.'

Another factor may have played a part in making her turn from writing books to the world of farming. Back in 1911, she had begun to be irritated by the late arrival of her royalty cheques, and complained to Harold Warne, who had been handling her affairs since Norman's death, 'I must confess I sometimes regret the times when cheques were smaller but punctual.' In April 1917, all her worst suspicions were confirmed. Harold Warne was arrested and sent to prison for forgeries totalling £20,000. He had embezzled most of the publishing money and spent it on himself, largely in the pursuit of his hobby, fishing.

LEFT: Cows at Manesty. Beatrix took a lively interest in cattle as well as sheep, and specialised in the Galloway breed.

Another brother, Fruing, took over the firm and perhaps surprisingly, Beatrix decided to stay with them. She felt loyal to the company, despite what Harold had done, and to the family, with whom she had always remained very friendly. The firm was reconstructed and emerged in 1919 as 'Frederick Warne and Co. Ltd.'. The word 'Limited' was added to protect authors and employees against any future financial fiddling. (It is a vital word for all collectors of Beatrix Potter first editions, which includes my humble self. If you come across an early copy without the word 'Ltd.', then you know it's pre-1919. Not necessarily a first edition, because, alas, identifying those is a study in itself.)

Beatrix had given Warne *Appley Dapply's Nursery Rhymes* in 1917, after a four year gap, just to get them started again. More nursery rhymes came in 1922, *Cecil Parsley's*, but apart from the *The Tale of Little Pig Robinson* much later, in 1930, there was never another real new story for Warne. Old stories and illustrations were re-hashed, in the form of various painting books and, in 1929, *Peter Rabbit's Almanac*. They kept pressing of course. In 1921 Beatrix was so fed up that she wrote to them, 'You don't suppose I shall be able to continue these d...d little books when I am dead and buried!! I am utterly tired of doing them and my eyes are wearing out. I remain with kind regards and very moderate apologies, yours sincerely, Beatrix Heelis.' So that was that. Exit B. Potter. Hello Mrs Heelis. How's the stock getting on? Very well, thank you. Growing all the time. But I can't stop now. Must go and muck out the barn.

Beatrix had quickly acquired three little farms around Sawrey to expand and protect her Hill Top property, but in 1924 she started a series of much bigger, more ambitious property deals. She bought Troutbeck Park Farm, near Windermere, a very valuable hill farm of some two thousand acres set in spectacular countryside. The sheep and the farm buildings that came with it were in poor condition, but she worked hard to improve them. She continued buying on that scale from then on.

RIGHT: Troutbeck Park Farm, at the head of the Trout Beck Valley. Beatrix loved this area, writing in 1942, 'In the calm spacious days that seem so long ago, I loved to wander on the Troutbeck Fell. Sometimes I had with me an old sheep dog, "Nip" or "Fly"; more often I went alone. But never lonely. There was company of gentle sheep, and wild flowers and singing waters.'
BELOW: Sheep at Troutbeck Park

ABOVE: *An old wash-house at Troutbeck Park Farm*
LEFT: *Monk Coniston, the house. Beatrix Potter managed the whole Monk Coniston estate for the National Trust.*

Her grandest purchase of all occurred in 1930 when she secured the Monk Coniston estate, four thousand acres going from Little Langdale to Coniston, which included such well-known Lakeland farms as High Yewdale and Tilberthwaite. On the day of the sale, she mentioned in passing to a friend that she and Willie were just going to look at a few fields. Monk Coniston also included Tarn Hows, today Lakeland's single most popular chunk of landscape, at least it is generally considered the most-visited beauty spot of them all. No entrance fees are taken, so no one knows exactly how many turn up, but it has been estimated that in a good year, one million folks come to gape and wander round the 'tarns', originally small and swampy little lakes, but later nicely landscaped.

As a farmer, Beatrix was doing two things, which went hand in hand. She was trying to make a decent return on her capital by working all the farms in what she considered was the most economic manner, but she was also preserving them, repairing eighteenth-century buildings, keeping up the best of the old customs of the hill farmers, as well as protecting the countryside for future generations to enjoy.

She had been greatly influenced by her friend Canon Rawnsley in all her preservation activities. So much so that she offered to sell the National Trust half of the Monk Coniston estate, some two thousand acres, for the sum she had paid for it, with the promise that they would get the other half free on her death. The Trust accepted with delight, but asked her in the meantime to manage the first half for them as well. She might have been an off-comer, a middle-aged woman from a non-farming background, but she was now accepted as sufficiently experienced to act as farm agent.

Beatrix had gone round all the fields of her little local Sawrey farms on foot, working personally with her tenant farmers, but as her estates grew she bought a car. It was a brand new Morris Cowley and she used her mother's footman, Walter, as chauffeur. She still mucked in, though, went barefooted to wade becks, helped with the hay-making, got down into drains to work out why they were blocked. Despite the chauffeur-driven car, she looked the part exactly, in her clogs, her old shawl and her apron made of rough sacking. She said she

LEFT: Geese at Newlands
BELOW: A sheepdog at Skelgill Farm, Newlands. Beatrix Potter drew the farm as Lucie's home in The Tale of Mrs. Tiggy-Winkle.

was at her happiest when with her cows and sheep, pigs and horses, poultry and rabbits.

'I have just come in after a rough two hours search for some sheep and lambs with a boy – the old man being poorly,' so she wrote in a letter in 1918. 'We got them, so that is done with . . . Somehow when one is up to the eyes in work with real animals it makes one despair paper-book animals.'

Was Mrs Heelis any good as a farmer, or was it just a case of money and enthusiasm talking? Her letters show an enormous regard for detail, pointing out the right materials to get, which suppliers would best do the job and who to avoid, and she kept all her farm tenants and managers up to scratch. A lot of her business was done for altruistic reasons, so her commercial success is hard to gauge. She would often buy property because she had heard rumours that bungalows were going to be built on it, or a new estate which would ruin a treasured view. She aimed at keeping the old farms very much as they were, running them independently and not amalgamating in the modern manner as most of the rest of England was doing.

Lakeland farms have always been small, even in the lusher, easier pastures of the valley bottoms. There's been a tradition in Central Lakeland of 'statesmen', yeoman farmers, often owning only between fifty and a hundred acres, running the farm themselves with only their families, perhaps taking on a hired man in the season. They are proud and

independent, getting on with their isolated lives, untouched by national dramas or wars outside Lakeland, even outside their own little valleys. It's only on the fringes you have the big estates and the gentleman farmers, the squires and the lords. On the hill farms, they're all workers, and dress accordingly for their working days, just as Mrs Heelis did. They also take time to accept people, weathering them in. First you summer them, then you winter them, then you might say hello. Cumbrian farmers take their time. It's not done to be nosey or forward with strangers.

LEFT: *Chickens at Threlkeld*
FAR LEFT: *Hay bales near Greystoke*
BELOW: *Traditional implements at Castle Farm, Sawrey, where Beatrix and William Heelis lived after their marriage*

ABOVE: *The Tyson family, who farm at Troutbeck Park*
RIGHT: *Cows in the Newlands Valley*

Beatrix experienced two World Wars as a farmer, putting up with all the restrictions and paperwork, rationing and shortages, but still obviously enjoying it. It was a learning experience for farming folk of every sort. Around 1940, she wrote to a friend, 'What with shortage of petrol and flu, farming is a bit of a problem. But keep smiling!' She finished the letter with a little cartoon drawing of herself and the wartime motto repeated below, 'Keep Smiling!'

Today, there are further problems local farmers have to put up with, which she could never have imagined. Radiation is one, either the ever-present worry that something nasty will fall out from nearby Sellafield, or from a nuclear plant thousands and thousands of miles away, like Chernobyl. Who could have imagined in Beatrix Potter's time that the lives of sheep farmers in Cumbria could be influenced or even ruined by a nuclear accident in the depths of Russia which would not allow them to sell their own lambs for fear of poisoning the population and themselves? That was what happened in 1986.

LEFT: *The spinning gallery at Yew Tree Farm, one of the Monk Coniston estate farms managed by Beatrix Potter for the National Trust. In 1938, she wrote to the National Trust agent: 'I think Yew Tree is worth more than £50 (the yearly rent), having a farm-house adapted for visitors and teas . . . I am afraid Mrs Atkinson has proved disastrously unsuited. Her husband has hardly given the place a fair trial yet, but there is no getting away from domestic limitations.'*
BELOW: *Yew Tree Farm*

In general however, the lives of hill farmers are not greatly different today, except that there are fewer of them. The hill farmer faces the inflexibility of the farming system open to him, as opposed to the lowland farmer who can follow production and marketing trends and adopt more profitable methods.

Cumbria is still primarily a livestock county as opposed to an arable. You don't see miles of wheat, as in East Anglia, just a few acres of barley perhaps round the luckier farmsteads. They grow animals in Cumbria, not crops. There are over a half a million cattle and one and a half million sheep. A good proportion of these cattle are dairy, some one hundred and fifty thousand, with the rest raised mainly for beef.

In Mrs Heelis's day, you could buy fresh milk from almost every little farm, and many did their own bottling and delivering. Now there are government health rules to restrict all that and milk is

BELOW LEFT: Fell ponies and sheep at Heltondale. Beatrix wrote in a letter to her cousin, Caroline Hutton, 'Our grand old local breed, the fell pony, has had a narrow escape, what with the government grant being withdrawn and the temptation to breed Clydesdale cross foals.'
BELOW: Cattle grazing at the top of Kirkstone

collected from the farms by bulk tankers and sent to local large scale dairies and creameries. (These lorries can be right brutes, should you chance to meet one on the narrow farm roads.) With all these changes, the average yield in milk has doubled since the war, while the number of full time workers employed on all Cumbrian dairy farms has greatly reduced, by about eighty per cent.

Dairy cattle were at one time mostly Dairy Short-horn. Now they are predominantly the higher-yielding black and white Friesian, plus some Ayrshire. Amongst the beef cattle, there's a new breed Beatrix would simply not recognise, the Charolais, which were first introduced from France in 1961 and are now very well established. They grow more quickly and are much bigger than the traditional Hereford. Other exotic cattle now being accepted are Limousin and Blonde d'Acquitaine. Cumbrian farmers have become very proud of their new stock, if not quite so sure about pronouncing their names.

The lowland Cumbrian farmers, especially those with cattle, have to battle with EEC regulations,

endless changes in subsidies and allowances. This of course is a penalty you pay if you try to work the system and keep up to date with profitable or fashionable lines. Hill farmers, who raise only sheep, just have to groan and bear it.

Ten years ago they were all quite pleased, as agricultural land everywhere was rising in price and they felt that whatever happened, they were sitting on capital, even if their income was weak. But at the present time, land prices have collapsed. Fields worth £2,000 an acre in 1978 are worth half that ten years later, sometimes as little as £600 or £700 an acre. (I know this, alas, as I bought thirteen acres with my cottage near Caldbeck in 1978, then sold all my fields at a large loss in 1987 when we moved to a

LEFT: Ruminating in the Newlands Valley
BELOW: Slag heaps at Tilberthwaite, on the Monk Coniston estate

house at Loweswater. Serves me right of course, but it's hard luck on the farmers.) Subsidies make nonsense of so much of modern farming, as farmers will rush into or out of milk production, encouraged by government or European policies, then end up over-producing stuff which no one wants. But what else can they do? They don't all like doing bed and breakfast or farmhouse teas – that's not man's work.

ABOVE: High Tilberthwaite

ABOVE: A wall made out of slabs of stone at Belmount
ABOVE RIGHT: Belmount

Mrs Heelis was fortunate as farmers go, with some family income behind her and her royalties flooding in. She could always turn her hand to one quick way of raising money, without having to put paying guests in the front parlour at Hill Top, or sleep with Willie in the spare room at Castle Cottage. (I know one hill farmer at Whelpo who sleeps in the bathroom with his wife when the trippers arrive, but then he does have a rather large, circular bath.) She still did sketches and watercolours for her own amusement, and when she was strapped for ready cash, she could find eager buyers, as in the old days. In 1927 there was a desperate call from the National Trust, who urgently wanted to buy a strip of land along the shore of Windermere, at Cock-

shott Point, to save it falling into the hands of a speculative builder. Beatrix had no cash at that precise point, all her funds being invested as farming was in one of its regular doldrums, so she knocked off fifty signed copies of a Peter Rabbit painting and sent them to an American contact, the editor of a magazine called *The Horn Book*, with instructions that they should be sold at one guinea each, all proceeds to the National Trust Appeal. She had to produce more, such was the demand, and £104 was in the end presented to the National Trust.

In 1928, another American visited Beatrix Potter, a publisher called Alexander Mackay from Philadelphia. She had been writing a much longer story for older children, and in 1929 this book, *The Fairy Caravan*, was published in America. The style of illustration was different from the *Peter Rabbit* books, but the settings were again mostly from around Sawrey and Hawkshead. It has never had the same success or popularity, in Britain or America, as her earlier work.

The proceeds from this last book went into further fields and farms. Like ashes to ashes, dust to dust, or should we say soil to soil, Lakeland love was being recycled. The local countryside had been Beatrix's inspiration, motivation and model. In turn, she used the profits from her work to buy more land, which she wanted ultimately to be preserved for everyone. She gave back far more than she took out. Riches to riches, perhaps.

Sheep

A sheep is a sheep is a sheep. Or so you might think, if you'd never seen one before at close quarters. There are forty different commercial breeds in Britain however, and not only do they come in all shapes, colours and sizes, with varying strengths and weaknesses, they have their differing personalities, as any shepherd will tell you. Beatrix Potter knew from an early age that rabbits were as varied as humans; she could definitely tell the difference between B. Bunny and P. Rabbit in character and appearance. She also knew that hedgehogs, mice, squirrels and ducks, all came with individual markings and personalities. Had she not loved and tended them for years in her nursery? Sheep, however, were something new. Even in the best-regulated Victorian or Edwardian nurseries, not many of the little darlings kept lambs under their beds. What would Nanny have said?

When Beatrix bought Hill Top, she not only bought a seventeenth-century farmhouse with a few fields and her sitting tenant farmer, Mr Cannon, she found she had acquired sixteen sheep as well. They were all Herdwicks, a native Cumbrian breed. Sawrey and its surrounds has rather lush pasture, mainly neat fields of lowland soil with a few rolling, gentle hills; nothing hard or barren, like the tops of the high fells where Herdwicks usually graze. Perhaps Mr Cannon had them because he liked them, or he'd got them cheap, or more likely he was fattening them up to sell at a reasonable profit. Herdwicks are a breed peculiar to the high

ABOVE: *Herdwicks, daubed with rud*
LEFT: *A magnificent horned tup at Skelgill Farm, Newlands*

fells of Cumbria, surviving where ordinary sheep would never live. The hill farmers who breed them usually sell them on to the farmers in the valley bottoms, who can provide better feeding, unless they have a few reasonable, grassy fields themselves, round their farmhouse, the 'inbye' land as they call it. Most farmers with top class land, then and today, would not concentrate on Herdwicks. They don't grow very fat. Their wool is considered rather coarse. And they don't give you a lot of lambs. A Herdwick ewe is only about sixty per cent sure to give you a lamb, whereas a Swaledale, also a

BELOW LEFT AND RIGHT: Sheep in the wintry Newlands Valley

hardy sheep, manages to be ninety per cent sure of reproducing. You should see, of course, what Herdwicks have to survive on for most of their life. You'd find it rather hard to get fat, grow wool, let alone produce babies, shivering at two thousand feet and trying to eat scree.

Beatrix Potter became captivated by Herdwicks, passionate about them, dotty even, deciding they were the breed she'd been born to battle for. Guess who encouraged her in all this, who helped her devote her farming life to Herdwicks? Canon Rawnsley of course. (How neat that his first name

should have been Hardwicke.) Not content with fighting to keep the Lake District free of nasty trains and horrible water boards, campaigning to preserve the Lakeland dialect and countryside, reviving the tradition of bonfires on mountain tops to celebrate national events, speaking out against the fashion for naughty postcards, and traipsing Cumbria to interview anyone who had known Wordsworth, he was also into sheep. In 1899 he founded the Herdwick Sheepbreeders' Association to encourage an interest in the breed and help re-establish it. Still going strong to this very day.

Herdwicks have been on the high fells of Cumbria for centuries. There is an oft-repeated legend, which still appears in countless tourist books, that they first arrived as a result of being shipwrecked from a boat off Ravenglass during the invasion of the Spanish Armada, four hundred years ago. An attractive notion, so why spoil it, except that a remarkably similar legend survives in Wales, to explain their Blackface sheep, and also in Ayrshire, to explain their cows. On the Isle of Man, it accounts for the Manx cat. Spanish boats did get shipwrecked in strange places, but why would a man of war carry sheep? They'd come to fight, not settle. And would sheep from sunny Spain turn out hardier than the native Cumbrian breed? (Goats, perhaps. You see goats in the Iberian peninsula being dragged along the most unpromising terrain.) A more likely theory has it that Herdwicks are very much older and arrived with the Norsemen. You're always pretty safe in Cumbria to blame the Norsemen. Most of the dialect and place names come from Norse. When the Norsemen arrived, Central Lakeland was a wooded wilderness. Clearances were made, sheep were put out to grass above the tree line and shepherds patrolled their patch, to protect their flock: hence 'herd wykes'. The earliest known record of the name is in the twelfth century, when the monks of Furness Abbey had their own flocks of 'herdwykes'.

RIGHT: Sheep among the scree high on Bowscale Fell

LEFT: Ewe and very young lambs
BELOW: Sheep shearing at High Tilberthwaite

There is an even cleverer theory, based on some recent finds at Vindolanda, a fort on the Roman Wall not far from the Cumbrian border. Excavations have dug up some material made from the characteristic hairy Herdwick wool. Could the Herdwicks have been there since Roman times, or even earlier, farmed by the Ancient Brits before the Romans arrived? In that case, the Norse might have taken them back to Scandinavia, rather than brought them here.

ABOVE: *The barn at Troutbeck Park Farm*
LEFT: *Sheep, waiting to be shorn, at High Tilberthwaite*

RIGHT AND BELOW: Shearing at Troutbeck Park. Beatrix Potter was always much occupied with the management of her various flocks. In 1930, she wrote to Caroline Hutton, 'I wish I had sold my wool. It dropped from £9 3s 4d to £4 3s 4d and now it is not wanted even at that price and I am afraid of rats getting into the heap, 1600 fleeces is a big stack!'
FAR RIGHT: Three generations of a farming family – the Birketts and the Wilkinsons at High Tilberthwaite

Let's agree Herdwicks have been here for a long time and their claim to fame has been their wool. During the time of the dissolution of the monasteries, there were bills and records of 'herdwycke shepcotes'. In Shakespeare's day, Cumbrian woollen goods were very well known and there's a reference in *Henry IV* to Kendal Green. John Peel's 'coat so grey' (on no account say 'coat so gay' or they'll batter you round Caldbeck) was probably made of the rough Herdwick wool. Textiles were the staple domestic industry for centuries in Lakeland, till the mills and spinning became industrialised and it all moved further south.

Herdwicks have always been grazed to maximise the poorer land, to get something out of all those wild crags and empty fell tops. Over the centuries, they have developed powers of survival unmatched by any other breed of sheep. They are capable of living – and lambing – at two thousand feet. The survival record is six weeks for a Herdwick lost and assumed dead in a snow drift. She eventually waddled out, complete with lamb, but virtually naked. The secret of their survival in snow is that they eat themselves. Well, not quite their own flesh. What they do is suck their wool, biting bits off and getting sustenance from it. It's partly the natural oils in the thick, coarse, shaggy wool which keep them going, and also all those fleas and insects.

Their other natural asset is their 'heafing' instinct. Like birds and salmon, they have a remarkable sense of direction, knowing where and when to return. Ewes will always return to the precise area of the fell which was their original home ground, or 'heaf', even if removed to the inbye land at lambing time. They take their own lambs to the same area, and the process continues. It means you don't have to fence them in, which is why they always appear wild, allowed to roam completely at will. It takes careful husbanding to avoid overcrowding on the available fell slopes, but if you get that right, the sheep can fend for themselves most of the year, apart from at lambing, dipping and shearing times.

ABOVE: After the shearing at Troutbeck Park
RIGHT: A flock by Wastwater

Each farmer has his own markings for his flock, a special clip to the ear and then a colour mark or 'smit' to the side of the sheep, usually a letter or some simple cross or stroke. Flock Books, containing all the different markings, are published every ten years or so. Despite their heafing instincts and their identity marks, some sheep still get lost or mixed up every year. There's a shepherds' meet at the end of every season when farmers and shepherds meet socially to compare notes, have a drink and a few songs, and swap back any mixed-up sheep. The meets always take place in pubs, going the rounds of a circle of pubs in the given area.

Economically, Herdwicks are never terribly profitable. Farmers who have good land or want an easier life will always try something else, depending on the state of lamb prices, government subsidies and other acts of Man and God which all farmers have to contend with. But if all you've got is the poorer land, or fell rights, up on the top, then your only hope of some return is a flock of Herdwicks.

The lambs are born practically black, but their coats get lighter as they grow older till they turn into a distinguished-looking rich cloudy grey. The rams are horned while the ewes are hornless. You don't see a lot of rams of course as not many are needed, so almost all are castrated from birth (rubber rings are fitted on their testicles which then drop off at about six weeks old). The life of the male is fairly short; they are fattened up for the slaughter-house either that first autumn or a year later. Very often they are sold on to farms lower down the fells, with better land, before going to market. Ewes can have a much more fulfilled life. Many have been known to survive for over twenty years, and by then may have produced around thirty lambs.

Beatrix Potter had to learn all the local Herdwick lore and language once she decided to become a specialist. A 'wether', for example, is a castrated male. A 'tup' or 'tip' is a mature male. A 'gimmer' is a young female sheep, until first mating, when she becomes a ewe. A 'hog' or 'hogget' is a young sheep of either sex, older than a lamb, who has reached his or her first autumn but not yet the first shearing. A 'shearling' has had his or her first shearing, usually at about fourteen months old. A 'draft ewe' is an old ewe, considered past her productive life and sold on to the lowland farmer, or straight to Carlisle to disappear into some supposedly meat pies, if there's any edible meat left on her after all those years out on the open fells. Herdwicks don't grow very fat or big, so per pound of meat they are not very economical.

You don't just have to name the sheep correctly – if you want to keep your head up at the auction sales, you have to know how to count them. Yet again, the strange counting words owe their roots to the Norsemen. 'One, two, three' is 'yan, tan, tether'. Then it goes on to 'mether, pimp, teezar, leezar, catterah, horna, dick'. After that, it's 'yan-dick, tan-dick, tether-dick', and so on. See, there is a logic to it.

Beatrix Potter's flocks of Herdwicks soon jumped in size, especially when she took over the Troutbeck Park Estate in 1924. After that, she had several thousand Herdwicks. She needed a new shepherd and hired one called Tom Storey who stayed with her, eventually based at Hill Top, for the rest of her life. He found that a lot of the new sheep were rotten with liver fluke, but Mrs Heelis researched the problem and invested in the latest treatments.

LEFT: *A ewe suckling her lamb, at Troutbeck Park*
BELOW: *Tiny lambs at Troutbeck*

Her letters to farming friends from then on are full of sheep and their ailments. Despite their hardy nature and ability to withstand the Cumbrian winters, Herdwicks, like all sheep, go down quite quickly when attacked by germs. These days they are dipped twice a year, if not thrice, and are regularly vaccinated against an assortment of viruses and internal parasites. A good shepherd these days is like a walking pharmacist, carrying all the dope and needles with him. Sheep have four stomachs, so there is four times the chance of getting stomach rot, and four times as many places for the maggots to hide and eat the sheep alive.

LEFT: *Sheep-dog trials at Loweswater Show*
BELOW: *Sheep penned together at Newlands*

ABOVE: Swaledales at Troutbeck Auction Mart
RIGHT: Herdwicks at Keswick Show
FAR RIGHT: Tup sales, Troutbeck Auction Mart

Beatrix once asked Tom Storey to cut off the head of the next lamb that died and skin it back to the shoulder, so that she could see the bare skull. She wasn't setting up as a vet but using the head to help her drawing, as she had done in her young days with the rabbit's skeleton. In that penultimate book of hers, *The Fairy Caravan* (1929), she was attempting to portray sheep, something she had always found hard. Tom saw her next day with the skull propped against a wall, sitting on a stone and sketching.

Tom Storey's greatest strength was as a judge of Herdwicks. He advised his employer at all the auctions and helped prepare her sheep for judging at exhibitions. In 1930 she was elected President of the Herdwick Sheepbreeders' Association, the first woman to hold that position in the organisation which her friend Rawnsley had founded.

I met Tom Storey in 1979, quite by chance. I'd been round Hill Top, worshipping at the shrine, and was wandering amongst the local fields when I came across this old man burning wellington boots. He was by then eighty-two, though he looked much younger, and remembered clearly those eighteen and a half years in which he had worked for Mrs Heelis as shepherd and farm bailiff. She gave him a copy of *The Fairy Caravan* when it came out, personally inscribed. 'You can read each of her books in twenty minutes,' he said, turning over the smouldering wellies. 'Yet she made all that money from them. I can't understand it.'

I asked him if she really was the expert on Herdwicks that all her biographers maintain. 'What could she know about farming, coming out of London? She liked Herdwicks, right enough. She'd look at no other, but she could make mistakes when judging them. I could give examples, but it wouldn't be fair, after all these years. I'll tell you just one. At Keswick Show one year we'd won everything and she was taking someone round. "These are the ewes we won with, aren't they Storey?" They weren't. They were Willy Rigg's. Ours were in the next pen . . . .

'She wasn't a bad farmer, I'll say that. We had our flaps. We differed over some things, but I didn't take much notice. I just got on with it. When you've gone through it all as a boy, you just carry on.

'I told her many a time she'd be better off having some cattle instead of all Herdwicks. She was losing money and I once got very worried. "Don't you worry, Storey," she told me. "It's only a hobby."'

Tom Storey died in March 1986, aged ninety. But there are still many other old shepherds and farmers in Lakeland who remember seeing Mrs Heelis at shows and auctions. It's surprising, talking to them, how few at the time knew where she got her money from, presuming it must be her husband's. She did keep her former persona very private.

'It was only when she died that there were these articles in the papers about the books she'd written,' says William Bowes, a retired Herdwick farmer from Broughton in Furness. 'She had plenty of money, though. I used to go to auctions with my Dad and if she was there and got her eye on a one for her flock, we couldn't knock her off. She was well advised. She was always strongest in the female championships.

LEFT: *Herdwicks, waiting to be judged, at Loweswater Show*
FAR LEFT: *Beatrix Potter and Tom Storey, with a prize-winning ewe*
BELOW: *Getting ready for judging at Loweswater Show*

ABOVE: *A curly-horned tup at Troutbeck Auction Mart*
LEFT: *The judging at Loweswater Show*

'I remember in 1937 going to a meeting of the Herdwick Breeders at Ambleside. In the Salutation, I think it was. I remember the year because I'd just passed my driving test and I drove me Dad there. I think the main topic that night was maggots. We didn't have such good dips in those days. She looked just as she looks in all those photographs, old tweed clothes and a dark cape. Her accent was what you'd expect. No, it couldn't be Cumbrian, could it? She spoke the way anyone would if they'd been educated by a governess. It was good English.'

The Herdwick Breeders' Association is still going strong today. The present secretary is Billy Bland, another retired Herdwick farmer, who lives near Millom. He remembers seeing Beatrix at the Keswick Ram Fair, in her shawl and clogs. 'They were always well-polished clogs. You wouldn't expect someone of her standing to wear clogs, not at a show. A farmer's wife might wear them at home, around the farm, but not outside, and certainly not at a show.'

Ten years ago, Herdwicks were in trouble and fast disappearing, so much so that they had begun to be described as a Rare Breed, in need of preservation. This was despite the efforts of the National Trust to protect them, following the pattern set down by Beatrix Potter. She always insisted when she bought over any farms that existing flocks of

ABOVE: *Gatesgarthdale, Honister Pass*
ABOVE LEFT: *A flock grazing above Hill Top*

Herdwicks had to be maintained. The Trust in turn insists on this, writing it into all their agreements. Because of their heafing instincts, it is advisable anyway. Flocks belong to a certain area, not to the tenant farmer, and he must hand on the same number when he retires. But on freehold, private land, many Herdwick farmers had given up. The post-war boom in artificial fibres had ruined the demand for wool and people anyway did not care for the coarse nature of the Herdwick coat.

The National Trust did some market research, analysed all the reasons for the decline in popularity of Herdwick wool, and started a marketing campaign which has had remarkable results. They investigated a way of taking the coarser strands out of the wool, and then commissioned leading knitwear designers to create new patterns for jumpers and jackets, gloves, scarves and hats, using the new yarn. I remember these fancy-looking designs appearing in all the National Trust shops round the Lake District, and listening to Christopher Hanson-Smith, then Regional Information Officer of the Trust, boasting about the revolution about to happen, while feeling very cynical. But it worked, if not exactly on the scale of a revolution. The success of the campaign was helped along by the desire to go back to nature in clothing, the ethnic, non-man-made look. One of the attractions of the Herdwick coat is that you can get two tones from it, suitable for tweeds, without the need for dyeing. You simply take wool from lambs, which is almost black, then mix it with the greyer wool from older sheep. The cloth never fades and lasts for decades.

'A friend of mine was in Keswick last week,' says Mr Bland. 'He saw there was a sale on at one of those Lakeland Skin Shops and he asked if they had any Herdwick stuff. Nothing left, they said. Anything under the counter then? No, they said. The Yankees have been in. They go mad for Herdwick tweed.'

Ten years ago, there were only a hundred members of the Herdwick Breeders' Association. Now there are one hundred and eighty. This doesn't mean to say there are more Herdwick farmers, just more interest. 'We have members all over. Even one in London, from a town farm in Finchley. When the word got around that we'd become a Rare Breed, people interested in sheep, such as farm parks, started having five or six. But it's the fashion for the wool that's done it, especially all this hand spinning that's started again.'

The commercial Herdwick farmers, with entire flocks, are all in Cumbria. Mr Bland has no idea how many individual Herdwicks there are, but the National Trust say their flocks number around twenty-five thousand animals. The Trust now owns one quarter of Lakeland, a great deal of it on the hills and fells, so one can guess that the total today is about fifty thousand. Not a lot, out of the one and a half million sheep in Cumbria. Swaledales are now the most popular, followed by Scotch Blackface, Rough Fell and a number of crosses. Herdwicks are still fairly rare, except on the open fells. Look out for their thick-set white faces, as opposed to the narrower, black face of the Swaledale, and the lack of horns amongst the ewes.

The Emperor of Japan has a Herdwick in his garden and most Japanese zoos have some on show. Until recently, a Tokyo department store kept one on its roof, all part of the export drive which has taken the good news about Herdwick wool and tweeds round the world. 'And don't forget the taste,' said Mr Bland. 'It's reckoned to be the best lamb. It was on the menu at Buckingham Palace for the Coronation.' Which Coronation was that, Mr Bland? 'Oh, every Coronation.'

The future of the Herdwick seems assured, at least for the moment, thanks to the inspiration of Canon Rawnsley, and the stout work and devotion of Beatrix Potter and the National Trust.

RIGHT: *Gathering sheep below Hindscarth, in the Newlands Valley*

Lakeland Sports and Shows

Lakeland sports are as old as Lakeland. Almost as soon as those Norsemen arrived, or those Romans unpacked, or if you prefer, the moment those Ancient Celts popped their heads out of the caves, they were racing each other up the nearest fell or throwing each other around or boasting that their particular animals were the greatest.

Beatrix Potter competed in the latter category. It was obvious from the moment she took such a passionate interest in her Herdwick sheep that she would want to display them to the world at large, at least those from the little world of her Lakeland community who considered themselves expert on the finer points of the Herdwick.

LEFT: The best wrestler's costume at Grasmere Sports
BELOW: Sheep at Keswick Show

By competing to win prizes, and then in due course becoming a judge herself, Beatrix found herself going the rounds of all the Lakeland shows and sports. The difference between the two is not always totally clear. A so-called Agricultural Show can also have races, between humans, animals or even people on bikes, while a sports can have a row of tents containing children's paintings or the local farmers' best sheep. The biggest events tend to be more specialised, concentrating on either agriculture or sporting activities, but the little local gatherings can contain anything and everything which the locals want to put in them. It was sheep which originally took Mrs Heelis along, but she was then caught up in the whole panoply and came to enjoy and understand all the activities. As for Willie, being locally born, he already knew most of the jargon, and as an enthusiast, he had taken part in many local sporting activities, for his own pleasure and recreation, rather than as a public competitor.

ABOVE: Industrial tent, Loweswater Show
RIGHT: Shepherds' crooks at Patterdale Sheep-dog Trials
BELOW: Cabbages, Loweswater Show

From her earliest visits to the Lake District, Beatrix had loved the local shows. In 1896 she first chanced upon the Hawkshead Show. '*Wednesday, September 2nd.* Hawkshead Show. Our dear fat friend got nothing. The second favourite and one of the cows took highly commended. The only prize *we* took was for *common turnips*, which little Mr. James Rogerson seemed to think almost an insult. It was a sight to see that little man struggling with other people's pups. A row of them held with their tails to the judges, who prodded their broad backs.'

As well as seeing one of the big events, such as Grasmere Sports or Ambleside Sports, any visitor to Lakeland should also catch one of the smaller ones, hidden away in the valleys, to experience the real atmosphere of the Lake District. In doing so you'll come across several activities which are pure Cumbrian, unknown in this form anywhere else in the world. They're pure in the sense that they have been unaltered for centuries and also pure in the sense of being uncommercialised. Local firms do take ads in the programmes, put up prizes and display their names on the tents, but so far the sports and shows have not been taken over by big sponsors. Grasmere Sports is still called that, and not the Barclays Bank Sports or the Ford Escort Sports. (Nothing necessarily wrong with that. The Tate Gallery in 1987 had Ford's name splashed all over their publicity, as sponsors of the Beatrix Potter exhibition. Expensive ventures can need wealthy backers.) But so far the fell runners don't trot out onto the field with the logo of a lager on their shirts, wrestlers have not yet got their league named after a cigarette firm, and Herdwick sheep have still to parade round the ring advertising Bellamy's Meat Pies on their backsides. It might happen soon, of course. An event which can attract twenty thousand spectators is as worth sponsoring as many a First Division football match. Perhaps some of the organisers are in fact desperate for sponsorship money, and only waiting to be asked. We shall see. In the meantime, as I go round the shows every summer with my family, I like to think ah, isn't this lovely, isn't this unsullied, aren't you all proud to have Cumbrian blood in your bodies?

Cumberland and Westmorland is probably the most famous of all the native sports, a sight to be seen nowhere else outside the Northern Counties, and it has given its name to a style of wrestling. Every Cumbrian sports of any size has a 'wrustling' event, often for a world title which can amuse the visitor by its presumption. But it's not much dafter than the Americans having a World Series in which only they take part. Anyone can enter a Cumberland and Westmorland wrestling competition. Just take your jacket off and have a go. Then see what happens to you. It is much more technical than it appears and is not just a matter of brute strength. You start by clasping hands behind the neck and shoulders of your opponent, with your chin on his right shoulder. The first one to unclasp his hands, or touch the ground with any part of his body except his feet, is the loser. Very simple. There are basically no more rules. The skill is in twisting your opponent to the ground using your buttock as a lever. You often see little headlines in the *Westmorland Gazette*: 'Tom's Winning Buttock'.

RIGHT: Cumbrian wrestling at Grasmere Sports

The only drawback for the novice spectator is firstly trying to see and secondly trying to work out who's winning. It has to be said that the only way to really know what this wrestling's like is to take part. But you can always watch the referees, sitting on their haunches nearby, or admire the costumes which the wrestlers traditionally wear at the big events. They appear to be in underpants pulled on over their long johns, like Superman in a forgetful moment. These underpants are always beautifully embroidered by wives and girl-friends, and at big sports, such as the Grasmere one, there is always a competition for the best-dressed wrestler. Try to get as near as possible for this. The judge is often a County lady in her Barbour with her Sloaney daughter in a headscarf and their comments can be, well, absolutely priceless, as they examine the cod-pieces of these strapping agricultural labourers.

RIGHT: Judging the wrestling
FAR RIGHT: Embroidered wrestling costumes, from the front . . .
BELOW: . . . and from the back

ABOVE AND RIGHT: The Guides Race, Grasmere Sports

As an exciting public spectacle, fell running is more immediate and easier to understand; except they often call it the Guides Race, and you might be half looking for young girls in uniform. Most sports have running races, but these are unusual in being run up and down the nearest fell. At a sports like Grasmere, the field is a natural amphitheatre. With a good pair of binoculars you can see every step of the way, and feel good that you don't have to try clambering up the rocks and bracken, only to come down again.

Perhaps my favourite moment in all Lakeland sports though is the finish of the hound trail, that moment when all the dogs return. I can never distinguish one hound from another in the distance, but once they arrive into the final stretch, it is pure theatre. The owners go wild, shouting and whistling, making their private signs and noises, waving favourite foods, anything to will on their hounds to make one last effort. The dogs have such a funny, walloping, lolloping, galloping style, yet they seem to glide over walls and becks like the smoothest of hurdlers.

Hound trailing is really fox hunting without the fox, so no one could object to it as a blood sport. It's done in the summer off season; two men drag an aniseed-soaked cloth over the fellside for several

ABOVE: The hound trail, Loweswater Show
RIGHT, ABOVE: Following the hound trail, Patterdale Sheep-dog Trials
RIGHT, BELOW: The finishing line, Grasmere Sports

miles, which the hounds then have to follow. In the old days, there was quite a bit of fiddling; wicked owners would try to switch dogs or lay false trails (so who says Cumbrian sports have always been pure?) but now it is all well-regulated and controlled. There is also, unlike the wrestling, organised betting at hound trails. Can they possibly be utterly pure even now? Hmm, that does indeed smack of commercialisation, but I happen to enjoy the sight of the little local betting booths with umbrellas and boards, the rural bookies in their slightly out-of-date racy hats and jaunty tweeds, or just in their normal farm clothes, as many of them are only part-timers. Hound trailing is part and parcel of the big sports and shows but it also takes place on its own, in gatherings purely devoted to hound trailing. The participants seem to descend on a field and set up their tents and trailers as if they're at an impromptu meeting. It's like a secret ritual too, and you feel out of it if you wander in by mistake. Many of the smaller trails are not advertised but are

ABOVE: Hounds at Patterdale
LEFT, ABOVE: Prize-winning hounds and their proud owners, Grasmere Sports
LEFT, BELOW: Dogs in the crowd at Patterdale, unaffected by the excitement

arranged by word of mouth. The signs are usually little huddles of farmers, two or three together, miles from anywhere. They look rather furtive, standing around apparently doing nothing. Then you suddenly hear the yelps of the hounds in the distance, the men start rushing and shouting, and a flurry of sweating, lathering hounds throw themselves over a wall and across the path, usually at the most unexpected point. And there's always a stray hound, wearily arriving much later, trying to work out where to go.

LEFT: *Getting the best vantage point for judging the wrestling at Grasmere Show*
FAR LEFT: *Grasmere Sports*
BELOW: *Westmorland Show*

Fox hunting has its own Cumbrian peculiarities. The members and followers don't ride horses or wear red coats. They cover the fells on foot and only one person, the Huntsman, wears a red coat. It's a thriving sport and the followers can often number thousands, rushing round the narrow roads in their cars to get the best views. There are three main packs in central Cumbria. The local one for the Heelises was the Coniston Hunt, still going strong, which covers the area east of Windermere. The others are the Blencathra, Melbreak, Ullswater, Eskdale and Ennerdale, and the Lunesdale.

ABOVE: Meet of the Melbreak Hounds at the Pheasant Inn, Bassenthwaite
LEFT, ABOVE: Singing 'D'ye ken John Peel . . .' at Caldbeck, where the famous huntsman lived and died
LEFT, BELOW: The Huntsman of the Blencathra Hunt, Johnny Richardson, looking out over Bowscale Fell

Sheepdog trials are also very popular. Because of her interest in Herdwicks, Beatrix kept some good dogs which often took part in gatherings. Her main concern was always the sheep however, and she showed them regularly, year after year, at places like Hawkshead, Ambleside, Eskdale, Keswick, Loweswater and elsewhere.

'We had speeches at lunch, at the Hawkshead Agricultural Show,' so she wrote in 1930, the year she became President of the Herdwick Breeders.

'An old jolly farmer – replying to a toast – likened me – the president – to the first prize cow! He said she was a lady-like animal; and one of us had neat legs, and walked well; but I think that was the cow not me, being slightly lame. We had our pretty little Baa's at Ennerdale Show last week and yesterday at Keswick . . . The sheep have been very successful in the female classes; sixteen first prizes, and several shows to come.'

There is always a big tent at these shows for the members and committee, where families sit down at trestle tables and have a set ham-salad type lunch, plus a bar where the lads gather and swap stories. Beatrix, a non-drinker, quite liked the image of herself attending meetings and gatherings with all the local people. 'You would laugh to see me, amongst the other old farmers – usually in a tavern (!) after a sheep fair.'

I have a sequence of unpublished letters by her, none very important, in which she is making various arrangements with officials of the Loweswater Show, between 1930 and 1935. Mostly they are addressed from Castle Cottage but one is from Hill Top, which shows she did use the house from time to time as another office. In one letter she is thanking the secretary for a cheque she has received for five guineas. 'And also for the Fell Dales prize which they obligingly supplied in brown grease.' What on earth could that have been? Some sort of food wrapped up, or a joke because a pie or something like it perhaps had collapsed? In another letter she is offering a special prize for the next year's show. 'Not for female sheep; the committee will know what would be a suitable class.'

LEFT: Beatrix Potter, talking to Harry Lamb, then Secretary of the Herdwick Sheepbreeders' Association, at the Woolpack Show, Eskdale
RIGHT, ABOVE: The beer tent, Loweswater Show
RIGHT, BELOW: Rudding the sheep, Loweswater Show

In a letter of July 1931 Beatrix writes she has good gimmer sheep at present, but the 'best lamb has slipped her jacket, past recovery.' (Presumably this means her wool is coming off and looks tatty.) She says she has promised a challenge cup for the Eskdale Show, and something for Keswick, but is worried about the show season ahead. From her letter, it looks as if some sort of animal disease was raging the county.

'I don't know what will be done about the shows down here. The restrictions are still in force – and personally I don't want to go to Kendal, as one never knows. There has been anxiety in the Hawkshead district, as nobody seems to have been getting any cattle lately, not like a previous scare some years ago.

Yours truly, H B Heelis.

PS We will have a good try to keep that cup! The sheep are in grand form – if we are free to come.'

One of the unusual things when Herdwicks are shown in competitions is that they have make-up put on, as if they were Miss World competitors.

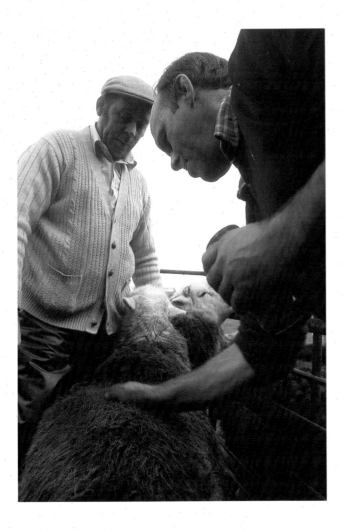

ABOVE LEFT: Sheep rudding, Loweswater
ABOVE RIGHT: Sheep at Westmorland Show
LEFT: Discussing the finer points of sheep-breeding,
Westmorland Show

This happens with no other breed of sheep, but has been a tradition for centuries in Cumbria. The dye is called Herdwick Red, or Rud, and is a sort of reddy powder that is brushed on to the sheep's coats to make them look more attractive, bring out the highlights and accentuate their positive points. It looks very strange to see the owners in their pens before the judging begins, fussing round the sheep, brushing and arranging their coats. Out on the fells, the animals soon go back to their normal dusty grey colour, apart of course from their smit markings.

*ABOVE AND RIGHT: Warcop Rushbearing, an annual
procession on St Peter's Day, originally to replace the rushes
in the village church
FAR RIGHT, ABOVE AND BELOW: Cattle at Skelton Show*

RIGHT: Pike fishing on Derwentwater. William Heelis loved fishing, and Beatrix would often accompany him.

Willie liked the social life that went with farming and the various shows and sports. He also enjoyed fishing, bowling, golfing and motorbiking on his own account. He was particularly keen on folk dancing and dragged Beatrix along too. There was a revival of this custom in the 1930s and it is still popular to this day. There are good accounts in Beatrix's letters of high jinks, songs and dances late at night. 'The stone-floored farm kitchen where we first danced "The Boatman" and heard the swinging lilt of "Black Nag". The loft with two fiddles where country dancers paced "The Triumph", three in arm under the arched hands. The long drive home in frosty starlight with a load of rosy sleepy village girls wrapped in rugs. . . . The plum cake and the laughter. Fat and thin, and high and low, the nimble and the laggard, the toddler and the grey-haired gran – all dancing with a will.' Beatrix did not actually do much dancing herself, preferring to sit on the sidelines and watch, but it obviously gave her a great deal of pleasure.

It might cost a bit of money to breed and show the best Herdwicks of the day, but there have always been lots of Lakeland activities which can be watched and enjoyed for very little.

ABOVE: A winter shooting party

Flowers, Fungi and Gardens

You don't immediately think of flowers when you think of the Lake District. It's the hills and lakes which come into your mind. Yet what about daffodils, which inspired Wordsworth's contribution to decades of classroom po-yums, one of the best known verses in the English language? Stop anyone and they'll give you the first line at least.

Beatrix Potter maintained an interest in all aspects of nature in the Lake District, not just in animals and farming activities, but also in the quieter, more private pleasures of fields, gardens, ponds, tarns and lake verges. As soon as she had acquired property in Sawrey, she got to work on her gardens, at Hill Top first and later at Castle Cottage. In the early days when she was planting the cottage garden at Hill Top, she was given many cuttings from the villagers. 'I have received more plants,' she wrote. 'It is a time of year when there are clearances and bonfires – I am receiving half the "rubbish" in the village gardens.' Her interest in gardening, the produce as well as the equipment, can be seen in all her little books. Just think of Mr McGregor's immaculate rows of vegetables, or the Flopsy Bunnies among the decaying marrows and the 'shot' lettuces in the compost heap. Then what about the wheelbarrows, waterbutts, sieves, flowerpots and watering cans, not to mention greenhouses and potting sheds? Beatrix was also very keen on soft fruits, loving to draw strawberries and blackcurrants, or wild fruit like elderberries, blackberries and crab apples.

ABOVE: *A watering-can and carnations, straight out of* The Tale of Benjamin Bunny
LEFT: *The herb garden at Acorn Bank*

She did many sketches and watercolours of wild flowers for her own pleasure, in particular bluebells, which she loved, and also foxgloves. Most well-brought-up Victorian girls did their share of nice flower paintings, but she tended to go for the more unconventional subject matter, looking into the weeds, studying the hidden plants. When she went with Willie on his fishing trips to Moss Eccles Tarn near their house, which she had bought and stocked with fish and water lilies, she sat in the boat and contemplated the fish jumping or the mallards playing on the banks, sometimes doing a few drawings.

ABOVE: Foxgloves, Fawe Park
RIGHT: Bluebells in Bishop Woods, above Sawrey. In The
Fairy Caravan, *the animals go through just such an enchanted*
wood: 'The ground beneath the trees was covered with
bluebells – blue as the sea – blue as a bit of sky come down.'

ABOVE: The lily pond, Fawe Park
LEFT: Snowdrops, Hutton-in-the-Forest

You don't immediately think of mushrooms when you think of Beatrix Potter. It's the sweet little animals and the roly poly fells which come into most people's minds. Yet she might well have devoted her life to fungi, if she'd had any encouragement, and only in recent years have experts realised just how extensively she studied and painted this apparently unattractive, unexciting subject. In her twenties and early thirties, it even looked as if she might make a career out of the study of various forms of fungi. The interest began on her holidays in Scotland and the Lake District, and continued back home in Kensington, when she visited the recently opened Natural History Museum. She even managed to cultivate spores, getting them to grow artificially in little dishes.

ABOVE: Hypholoma *fungus among the leaves, Manesty*
LEFT: A giant puff-ball
FAR LEFT: Coriolus *fungus, along a fallen branch*

LEFT: *Fawe Park Woods*

ABOVE: *A wall in the kitchen garden at Fawe Park*

ABOVE: The herbaceous border at Sizergh Castle
LEFT: The gardens at Muncaster Castle

To guide her in her scientific studies, Beatrix had a real expert in the family, her Uncle Harry – Sir Henry Roscoe, FRS, Vice Chancellor of the University of London. (He had married her father Rupert's younger sister, Lucy.) He helped to get the chemicals she needed for her experiments, and when she started seriously exploring the subject, he used his contacts at Kew Gardens to introduce her to the right people. In all, she made over three hundred drawings of fungi, formulated various theories, and was obviously sufficiently proud of the depth of her research to write to a cousin that it might be published. 'I have been drawing funguses very hard. I think some day they will be put in a book, but it will be a dull one to read.' This mild form of boasting never occurred with her children's stories, as she never thought they would take off until the surprise success of *Peter Rabbit*.

RIGHT: Ullswater, from Glencoyne
FAR RIGHT: A wild-flower bank at Sizergh Castle
BELOW: Buttercups in the Newlands Valley

ABOVE: Banks of heather on Skiddaw
LEFT: Ferns at Stagshaw Gardens

Her famous uncle's influence in the end did her little good. He opened doors at Kew, but all the experts there were rather horrible to her. She found them 'dry and cynical' and one of them, she said, appeared to have been dried out in blotting paper. The Director wrote a letter about her work to her uncle, which Sir Henry would not show her. Beatrix called the Director's action 'rude and stupid'. She described the Assistant Director as someone who had 'passed several stages of development into a fungus himself'.

She had told the Director at Kew that she had cultured between forty and fifty different kinds of spores, recording their development at six-hourly intervals and drawing each stage with the aid of a microscope. But his assistants did not believe her drawings and one of them objected to her slides. She warned them that her findings on lichens would be in all the books in ten years.

It was not just as an outsider, with no scientific qualifications, that she was upsetting the hierarchy by barging in with her own independent experiments and theories, but because she was a woman. She even prepared an academic paper, 'On the Germination of the Spores of Agaricineae'. She got it typed out and took it on the train herself to Kew to hand it over to the Director, but was too shy or scared to give it to him in person. The paper was eventually read, at least in title, in April 1897 at a meeting of the Kew scientists – but not by her. Women were not allowed to deliver papers or attend meetings.

Apart from the study of mushrooms and toadstools, she was also fascinated by insects and fossils and collected and painted them as well. Once her children's books got going, her scientific studies decreased, but the result of all this study can be seen in her books. Minor characters and objects are portrayed in naturalistic detail, such as Sir Isaac Newton the newt and the water beetles in *Jeremy Fisher*, Dr Maggotty the magpie in *The Pie and The Patty-Pan*, the Red Admiral butterflies in *Mrs. Tittle-mouse* and *Tom Kitten*.

The fungi research comes into *The Fairy Caravan* (1929), where Paddy Pig suffers from the hallucinogenic effects of toadstool tartlets. It's a wonder, in this present age, that no one has discovered any hidden drug messages in Beatrix Potter, though her mushrooms and toadstools are mainly used for sitting on, not eating, at tea parties or little meetings. Peter Rabbit of course drinks camomile tea, though this is a herb, not a so-called drug, unless you describe all teas and herbs as drugs.

After one of her earliest visits to Sawrey, Beatrix wrote in her *Journal*, 'I think one of my pleasantest memories of Esthwaite is sitting on Oatmeal Crag on a Sunday afternoon . . . and all the little tiny fungus people singing and bobbing and dancing in the grass and under the leaves all down below . . . and I sitting up above knowing something about them.'

'I am written out for story books,' so she wrote in a letter in 1934. 'And my eyes are too tired for painting, but I can still take great pleasure in old oak – and drains – and damp walls – oh the repairs. Such are the problems which occupy my declining years.' She used to tell friends in Sawrey later on that it was all those early years drawing fungi which really ruined her eyes.

In 1934 Beatrix gave a large number of her watercolours and drawings of fungi, mosses, lichens, fossils and architectural studies, plus a massive bundle of show catalogues she had kept over the years, to the Armitt Library in Ambleside. This was a subscription library, founded by three rather Bronte-ish ladies, Mary Louisa, Annie Maria and Sophia Armitt, who were amateur writers and artists. They concerned themselves with good works in Lakeland, encouraging studies of local history, geology, poetry and painting. Willie Heelis had been the solicitor for the library since its foundation in 1912, and on her marriage, Beatrix became a member. She greatly approved of its aims, as of course did Canon Rawnsley. Other donors to the library over the years were Arthur Ransome and G. M. Trevelyan.

RIGHT: Herbaceous border, Dalemain

ABOVE: *The kitchen garden at Fawe Park. In* The Tale of Benjamin Bunny, *old Mr Bunny imprisoned the cat in these very greenhouses.*
LEFT: *Topiary at Hutton-in-the-Forest*

The library is still going in Ambleside, and has almost three hundred of Beatrix Potter's fungi illustrations, as well as other studies and her reference books. In 1966, a professional mycologist, Dr W. P. Findlay, chanced to see a display of Beatrix's fungus paintings and was so impressed by them that he used fifty-nine in a book, *Wayside and Woodland Fungi*, which was published by Warne in 1967. So her little boast, made all those years ago, came to pass. And experts now do accept that Beatrix Potter's assertions about lichens (maintaining that they were dual plants) were basically correct.

You can visit the Armitt Library today at Mill Cottage, Ambleside, but you have to become a member first, as it's still a private Trust. The Library is currently appealing for funds to rehouse and conserve its many treasures, including its Beatrix Potter fungi drawings, the largest collection of these in the world. It is nice to know they are still in the Lake District, when you think how much American and Japanese museums or collectors would pay for them today, not to mention the V and A or the Tate in London, if they had the money.

You can of course go freely around Hill Top as a member of the public, and see Beatrix's gardens, and also visit Lingholm on Derwentwater where her love of Lakeland flowers and gardens began. There are many other fine gardens which are all open to the public, such as Acorn Bank near Penrith or Stagshaw Gardens near Ambleside. Brantwood, Ruskin's old home, has an interesting wood. Lakeland does have some magnificent stately homes too – they're not all miniature masterpieces like Hill Top – and most of them have excellent gardens, particularly Levens Hall near Kendal with its topiary, Dalemain near Penrith, Holker Hall at Cark in Cartmel, Sizergh Castle near Kendal and Hutton-in-the-Forest near Penrith with its fine trees. Or look out for the daffs on the slopes above Ullswater at Gowbarrow Park. Still there, just as Mr Wordsworth saw them.

Tourism

Is Beatrix Potter the biggest single crowd-puller in Lakeland today? How can you possibly prove such a thing? And does it really matter? Well, in the Top Ten Lakeland Names League her home certainly gets the greatest crowds and her books sell in the greatest numbers (total so far, around sixty million copies). Whether visitors come to the Lake District because of her, as opposed to Wordsworth or Arthur Ransome, is harder to check. Brockhole, the Lake District National Park Centre, is the single most-visited building of the area, getting more visitors than Hill Top or Dove Cottage put together, but once inside, you'll find that one of their most successful displays is devoted to Beatrix Potter.

LEFT: *Easter crowds at Waterhead*
BELOW: *The Beatrix Potter industry: a shop window in Ambleside*

ABOVE AND RIGHT: Two of the more peaceful sports Beatrix Potter would have approved of: ballooning over Derwentwater, and canoeing on the lake

ABOVE: *Repairing boats before the summer season at Bowness on Windermere*
LEFT: *The rewards of walking: looking down on the Newlands Valley from May Crag*

But can you compare a mere mortal with natural wonders like Ullswater or Helvellyn; surely they are the real attractions for the thirteen million people a year who visit Lakeland? Possibly. The only trouble with assessing the popularity of those places is that no one is doing a head-count. We only know about beauty spots where official estimates have been made, such as, well let's choose one almost at random: Tarn Hows, always reputed to be the honeyest honeypot. And as we know, it is thanks to B. Potter that we can visit it today. But there's nothing to be gained by trotting out spurious statistics to prove some pointless point. Lakeland wonders are above such vulgar comparisons.

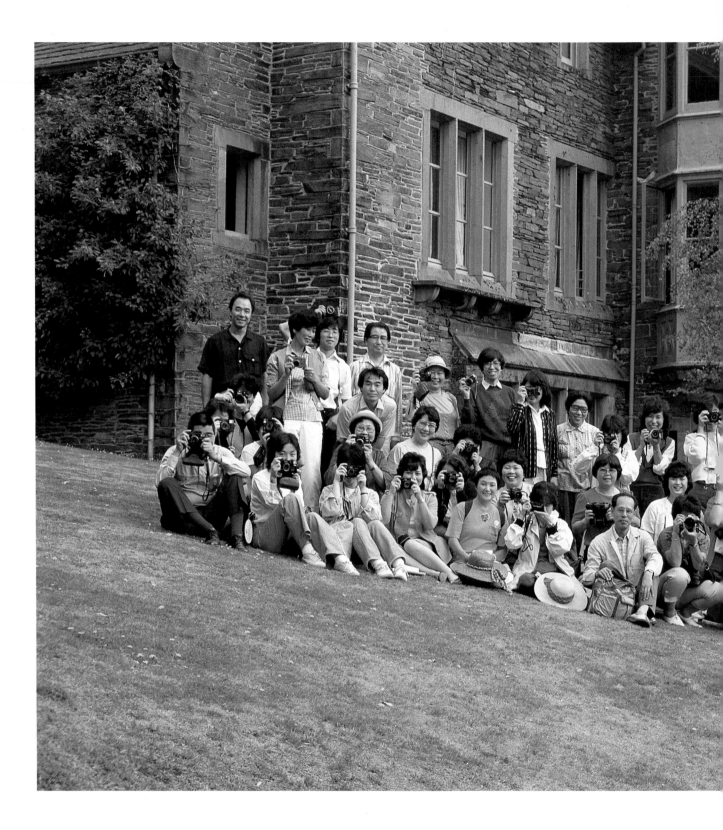

One of the most remarkable things about Beatrix Potter is that despite her enormous fame, which was bound up with a known and recognisable locality, and despite the fact that she was a very keen businesswoman when it came to marketing her own products, she remained a totally private citizen throughout the whole of her life. Look in any newspaper library or file, as I have done many times, and you will not find any interviews with either B. Potter or H. B. Heelis. Nothing. Not even a cosy quote for the *Westmorland Gazette* or the *Cumberland News*. I can think of no other comparable author who has ever gone to such lengths to remove him or herself from the public eye, or the eye of his or her readers. In our own time, Graham Greene is a pretty private person, but over the years, his cuttings file has become quite thick with personal interviews, given at fairly regular intervals. Wordsworth devoted his life to poetry, and refused all inducements to write for the newspapers (unlike his friends Coleridge, Southey and De Quincey), even though at times he desperately needed the money. But once fame came, with the mantle of Poet Laureate, he rather enjoyed lording it at London dinner parties; at home at Rydal he graciously talked to the rubber-necks who gathered at his gate. And if he wasn't in, one of his staff often flogged the tourists locks of his hair, so they should at least have something of the Great Man.

LEFT: Forty-two Japanese admirers of Beatrix Potter at Fawe Park

Beatrix Potter would have none of this. It was as if she was denying her previous existence as Beatrix Potter, the author, and would only admit to Mrs Heelis, wife and farmer. As the ultimate tourist attraction, she made it her business to repel tourists who came to goggle at her, rather than the country-side.

This mania for privacy rather rebounded on her in the 1920s when the newspapers of the day started carrying stories about Sidney and Beatrice Webb, the famous socialists and Fabians. When it was discovered that Mrs Webb's maiden name was Potter, someone jumped to the conclusion that she must be Beatrix Potter, author of the well-known children's books. Once one newspaper had made the mistake, others copied. The real Beatrix was furious at the very idea of being mistaken for such an unattractive person; Willie was pretty upset as well. They were both good conservative, old-fashioned people of course, not at all in tune with these new radicals. But how could she correct the mistake, without drawing attention to herself? She described the dilemma in a letter to her publishers, Warne, in 1924.

RIGHT: Walking along Saddleback

'I usually take no notice, as even the insult of being mistaken for Mrs S. Webb is preferable to publicity. But if the Webbs are going to become prominent along with our new rulers, the error had better be contradicted; for I do not think that nice old-fashioned people who like my books would like them quite so much if they believed them to be of socialist origin . . . Mr Heelis is much edified by the portraits of Mr and Mrs Webb on the front page of the *Herald*; he says that it is adding insult to injury to suggest that Miss Beatrix Potter is married to "such a little animal"! He thinks it wants stopping. I should not like my real name to have to come out; if the thing unfortunately spreads, I think the best contradiction would be to get photographed along with a favourite pig or cow and get it inserted in some more genteel newspaper? I had lately a pig that continually stood on its hind legs leaning over the pig stye, but it's hanging up, unphotographed and cured now.'

It is perhaps surprising that Beatrix was never tempted to please the tourist trade by producing any

BELOW LEFT: A break for chips in Ambleside
BELOW: Strolling along the lakeside at Waterhead

guide books, or even just a collection of water-colours of local views, celebrating the beauties of her particular part of Lakeland; but this would have meant drawing attention to herself. Most writers who have lived in the Lakes for any length of time have usually succumbed to this temptation, an excuse to pass on their thoughts and make a little extra money. Wordsworth was one. At a time when he was pretty hard up, he did some words anonymously for a series of watercolours by a Norfolk vicar in 1810. Later on, he re-wrote them and produced his

own *Guide to the Lakes*. The book proved an enormous success, running into many editions, and can still be bought today in a facsimile version. There's the well known story, first told by Matthew Arnold, about the clergyman who asked Mr Wordsworth if he'd written anything else – apart from his *Guide*.

In the end, Wordsworth fell to complaining about the hordes of tourists who were threatening to overwhelm the Lakes, bringing their vulgar ways with them, ruining his beloved landscape. One of the arguments he made (perfectly seriously) when he was campaigning against the Windermere railway was that the poor and ill-educated would not benefit 'mentally and morally' from the Lakes and would spoil the area for the educated classes 'to whom such scenes give enjoyment of the purest kind'. Wordsworth could at least say with some justification that in his lifetime the Lakes had been 'ruined'. Many people have said this since, and are still saying it, wanting the drawbridge pulled up the moment they become resident, alleging that the good old days have gone, that there are too many people walking the fells, climbing, camping or just hanging around in Bowness, guzzling ice cream.

RIGHT: Looking down on Brotherswater from the Kirkstone Pass

The arrival of the first tourists in Lakeland co-incided with Wordsworth's birth, in 1770. Until then, it had been left to the farmers and sheep; there is no recorded evidence any earlier of parties of trippers; certainly no proper books to help them. Adventurous gentlemen went instead to Europe for their scenery, to the Alps or the Rhine, imagining places like Lakeland to be full of rocks and possibly monsters. But, by the end of the eighteenth century, it had become the fashion to explore one's native heath: places such as Scotland and the Lakes. When the Napoleonic wars came along, much of Europe was cut off for British tourists anyway for many years.

The first Lakeland guides came out in the 1770s. They were written by Thomas Gray (of *Gray's Elegy*), by Thomas West, a Jesuit father, and by the Rev. William Gilpin, who was at least a Cumbrian, born near Carlisle. These are the classical guides, worth getting hold of today, if just for their illustrations. These early books warned of awful crags and frightening sights, recommending human guides to lead the way, but they also pointed out the high spots, the so-called 'picturesque' places, which all true visitors just had to see and experience. People like Gilpin listed 'stations' from which you could see the best scenery, with of course the use of the Claude glass that all good tourists carried. (This was basically a mirror which you looked into over your shoulder, turning your back on the actual view.) Then if you were suitably inspired, you got out your watercolours or your pencil, depending on what Gilpin thought was the best means of capturing the view from each station.

These guide books, plus Wordsworth's, brought visitors in by the thousands and wealthy Lancashire folks started building holiday or retirement homes in the Lake District. It was the advent of the railways in the 1840s however which brought in tourists by the millions. Major rows over the railways were finished by the time Beatrix Potter had established herself in Lakeland; Canon Rawnsley fought the last of them. The trains had an immediate and dramatic effect. Almost overnight, the little hamlet of Birthwaite became the booming Bowness and Windermere, virtually one town, the biggest in Lakeland. This particular line never got any further than Windermere; it never passed the garden gate at Rydal Mount, which was what Wordsworth had really feared, or got as far as Keswick, which was the original plan. Other Lakeland lines did get built: the Furness line which got to Coniston and the cross-Lakes line between Cockermouth, Keswick and Penrith. Both of those, alas, are now gone, and I personally miss them. A far nicer way to travel than dragging up the motorway, which is how eighty per cent of present-day visitors arrive in Lakeland.

Beatrix Potter was greatly annoyed by many of the activities of the tourists she saw around her. She disliked charabancs and worried about the problems they caused on narrow Lakeland roads. She was always on about the awful habit of 'gramophoning': people taking out their machines and playing records right in the middle of quiet beauty spots. (She should have lived till the age of the trannie, or worse, the ghetto blaster.) When she bought Tarn Hows in 1930, it was receiving thousands of visitors a year, and many of them, being very forward and cheeky, went swimming in hot weather. (As all Lakeland visitors know, the lakes are often warm enough to swim in, well, once every two years anyway.)

ABOVE: *Tarn Hows is just as popular today as it was in Beatrix Potter's time*

'Bathing is most perplexing,' so Mrs Heelis wrote. 'It seems cruel to refuse in hot weather, but they should not do it at the exposed end of the lake.' Then there were even hard-faced people who actually drove to the lake. 'I was displeased one hot summer to see people going from cars to the lake. It is so difficult with rules. The Miss Scotts took a gramophone to walse [*sic*] on the ice; a general habit of gramophoning and wirelessing would be a great nuisance.'

Another particular modern manifestation which really annoyed her was the aeroplane, the early flying boat variety which in 1912 was becoming very popular on Windermere. There was even the possibility of an aeroplane factory being built near Bowness Bay. 'There is a beastly fly-swimming sputtering aeroplane careering up and down over Windermere,' she wrote in a letter. 'It makes a noise like ten million bluebottles. It is an irritating noise here, a mile off. It must be horrible in Bowness. It seemed to be flying very well, but I am sorry it has succeeded. If others are built, it will very much spoil the lake.'

ABOVE AND RIGHT: The Gondola, *The National Trust's steam launch, on Coniston Water*

This particular subject gave rise to the only known occasion when she did come out in public and stick her head above her private parapet. (Thus disproving my earlier assertion.) She wrote a letter to *Country Life*, long and colourful, warning readers about the threat to Lakeland peace. She then got up a petition to protest against the factory, using her known name, Beatrix Potter, not Heelis, and was very pleased that the signatories included thirty-four doctors and nurses at the London Hospital. In the end, the aeroplane factory was never built.

Apart from that incident, her private life was very much her own, and she refused to see all newspaper people and writers who tried to doorstep her, as many did. She also refused to encourage ordinary readers, who might just arrive out of the blue having tracked down her lair. She kept her British fans at bay, though for some reason she was flattered by the occasional American who wrote or came to call. She was impressed by their quiet enthusiasm and knowledge of her works. It was as if some British critic had been horrid to her in the past. This was not the case, though naturally there were always people who greeted each new book by saying she had 'gone off'. (This happened as early as 1904 when a clever clogs in *The Times Literary Supplement* said that *Benjamin Bunny* was not such a good story as *Peter Rabbit* and that 'Miss Potter's fancy is not what it was'.) She must have known from her tremendous British sales that the natives did love her. Perhaps she was afraid of constant visits, whereas Americans or New Zealanders would not often come to Sawrey.

LEFT: Cross-country biking at Tarn Hows

Her contact with various American visitors, particularly a librarian from the New York Public Library, Anne Carroll Moore, resulted in her renewing work on several projects she had dropped. She finished off *Cecily Parsley's Nursery Rhymes* on Miss Moore's encouragement, and of course her penultimate book, *The Fairy Caravan*, was published first in America.

Despite her affection for Americans, she was not at all keen when Walt Disney, no less, wrote to her personally in 1936, asking for permission to film Peter Rabbit. 'My drawings are not good enough,' she commented. 'To make Silly Symphonies they will have to enlarge them and that will show up all the imperfections.' (It was not until 1971 that a film was made, *The Tales of Beatrix Potter*, Frederick Ashton's ballet version for EMI.)

Beatrix was not entirely inconsiderate towards general Lakeland tourists, having been one herself not so long ago. She always made allowance for their pleasure on her property, as long as they left her alone, and encouraged her tenants to provide bed and breakfast and teas, compensating them for any loss of agricultural income. At Yew Tree Farm, near Coniston, she offered some of her own surplus furniture to her tenant farmer, so that nice teas could be served in the parlour. Naturally she did get upset when visitors took too many liberties. 'I speak with feeling as a farmer as I have not forgotten the exasperation of seeing a party of large young women chasing over a succession of newly "cammed" walls in pursuit of mushrooms. I like to see them enjoy themselves – if only they would shut the gates when they come down.'

RIGHT: Climbing Skiddaw

There was even one species of British visitor whom she encouraged to stay on her property: the Girl Guides. She was doing them a favour as Mrs Heelis, farmer, not as B. Potter, letting them put up their tents in her fields around Sawrey and Hawkshead, or use her barns if the weather was bad. 'I have never received any rent; only an abomination called "slides" with which young people do up their hair; but unwholesome for cows, when subsequently eating hay beds; they also left buttons and paper in the hay. The dairy maid had to pick it over, being rewarded by the treasure trove, and was satisfied with her bargain.'

As ever, she describes these little events wittily, so you are never quite sure if she's being sharp and wry or just straightforwardly funny. The Guides became almost an annual feature from the late 1920s and she always looked forward to their visits. When one of the 1st Chorlton-cum-Hardy Guides became ill, she lent her car and chauffeur to drive her all the way home to Manchester. She offered ten pounds to hire tents, when it looked one year as if the Guides might not be able to afford to come, gave them autographed copies of her books, lucky girls, and even posed for their photographs. 'It is always a pleasure to help Guides and it brings its own rewards – for surely it is a blessing when old age is coming to be able still to understand and share the joy of life that is being lived by the young. If *I* slept in a tent, I might get sciatica . . .. I am delighted to have the photographs . . .. I can recognise many of the Guides. We have a laugh at M E and I ought to have had my fine new teeth in! I look a good-natured old body at all events.'

ABOVE: *Picnicking on Maiden Moor*
ABOVE LEFT: *Beatrix Potter and the Girl Guides at Hill Top*

That was another reason why she was able to remain so anonymous, unrecognised even as the wife of a successful solicitor. By dressing like an old farm yacker even when out and about in public places, in her clogs and apron made out of sacking, most people would pass her without another look. She seems to have been quite proud of looking like a real local. No one suggested it was deliberate. It was just that her mind was preoccupied more by farming affairs than by clothes.

One day, when coming home in the rain from the Windermere ferry, a real tramp walked with her part of the way. 'It's gay weather for the likes of thee and me, missuss,' said he. She often told this story against herself, roaring with laughter. All part of her successful attempt to repel tourists, and keep the non-farming world away.

Lasting Portraits

Canon Rawnsley's wife died in 1915, just two years after the marriage of Beatrix and William Heelis. There were those who thought that had Beatrix still been Miss Potter when he became a widower, well, who knows what might have happened? They had always been very close friends and the difference in age was only fifteen years. In fact Rawnsley remarried in 1918 and spent the last years of his retirement at Allan Bank, Grasmere, the 'new and abominable house' which at one time Wordsworth had rented, till the smoking chimneys drove him frantic. It is now owned by the National Trust.

Rawnsley died in 1920. His major and lasting epitaph will always be the National Trust, celebrating its centenary in 1995. But he will be remembered in Lakeland too for all his other interests, and for encouraging so many local activities, even though today many of them have been forgotten or superseded by new ideas or customs. The fine building which once housed the Keswick School of Industrial Art (founded by Rawnsley and his wife) is now an Italian restaurant, though the art nouveau overtones have been skilfully preserved. (It's just opposite what was once the home of Southey and Coleridge, Greta Hall, now part of Keswick School.) We have in our house somewhere a little award which my wife won when competing for the Rawnsley Shield, many years ago at Carlisle and County High School. The competition was for verse-speaking in public; I can't believe that it still exists today, in this comprehensive age.

ABOVE: A footbridge, Borrowdale
LEFT: Derwentwater

Rawnsley was the ultimate idealist, but one who did get things done, dragged new bodies into being. He believed in our basic goodness, and that we would all look after beautiful things if they were made available to us. Beatrix Potter was slightly more hard-headed. She favoured more regulations, realising that farm land needed protection and that the public could not be allowed free access everywhere. She believed that farmers and their stock came first, and knew that the public could at times be a bit of a nuisance, getting in the way of the workers, whom she considered were the real preservers of the landscape. She even kept an eye on the National Trust in those early decades, while managing the two thousand acres she had passed on to them, just in case they did anything she disagreed with (and they often did).

ABOVE LEFT AND RIGHT: Derwent Fells and Causey Pike. 'The vastness of the fells covers all with a mantle of peace.'

The arguments about this conservation balance still go on. Is it our land, we the citizens, regardless of where we live, only held in trust for us and our

descendents by the present 'owners'? On the other hand, can the millions just be allowed to come in and trample everywhere, damaging the landscape by all wanting to climb Catbells at the same time and by the same route? The joy of Lakeland is that you can usually escape the hordes in just half an hour, wherever you are, but increasingly you have to avoid the most popular spots at peak holiday times. I climbed Scawfell Pike recently with my family, a glorious six-hour walk before we got to the top, six hours away from all man-made roads and buildings. When we reached the summit, there was a queue. We had to wait patiently for our turn to clamber on the cairn.

Are farmers really any better than the rest of us at looking after our heritage? They poison the fields with chemicals, destroy hedges to make way for their machines, litter the dikes with empty plastic fertiliser bags, change round their stock and their fields to catch some passing EEC subsidy. It's nice to see Herdwicks still up there on those apparently barren fells, but how much are they helping our environment? They don't put a great deal back into the soil in the way of manure, as cattle do (the minerals they take from the land go into their coats); they crop so closely they can even cause erosion. I used to fight endless battles with the Herdwicks and Swaledales breaking into the garden I was trying to save at our cottage on the Caldbeck Fells. They will eat anything, as unchoosy as goats, destroying if not eating every new shoot on every possible sort of vegetation. In the end, the only things that survived in ten years were the gooseberries. Just too prickly for their voracious mouths.

The march of the Forestry Commission conifers has now ceased, at least on its former pattern and scale, and the Commission are now mixing their new wooded areas, which is much more pleasing on the eye. They have been widely attacked for their policies, and it is still fashionable to complain about regimented forests, but they can say that they are reclaiming hillsides worn away by nature and by sheep, providing a framework in which oaks can grow again and a shelter for flora and fauna which would otherwise not exist. The problem of achieving the right balance between farming, tourism and preservation in Lakeland will always be with us, and grows more expensive all the time. Pity the folks who have to try and work out the right policies.

Mrs Heelis was not too concerned with abstract theories about Lakeland conservation. She was a working farmer, with enough day-to-day agricultural business to keep her mind and body occupied. She also had family matters which required a lot of attention in her middle and later years: in the shape of her mum. After the death of her father, Beatrix managed to find a suitable home for her mother: Lindeth How in Storrs Park (it's now an hotel). It wasn't far away, just across the ferry on the other side of Windermere. Mrs Potter arrived in 1918, aged eighty, and settled in with four maids, two gardeners and a coachman-cum-chauffeur. For the next fourteen years she was ever-present, and ever a problem in Beatrix's background. They had never really got on, but that did not stop Mrs Potter continuing to exact tribute and attention from her daughter.

RIGHT: A rainbow over Keswick

ABOVE: Crummock Water

ABOVE: *Wastwater*

ABOVE: *Loweswater*
ABOVE RIGHT: *Hawes Water*

Beatrix would usually walk from Sawrey on visits to her mother, down to the ferry, then catch the boat across the lake, and walk to her mother's house – unless her mother sent her car to the ferry to meet her, which was not always the case. There were occasions when old Mrs Potter would refuse to see her, if they had had some sort of row or she had decided her chauffeur and car had more important jobs to do than pick up her daughter. Such as shopping. Every week her favourite maid, Lucissa, was sent into Windermere in the chauffeur-driven car to buy a penny apple – one and no more – which was needed to feed Mrs Potter's pet canaries. So if Beatrix's visit clashed with that arrangement, it took second place.

'My mother is refusing to die,' so Beatrix wrote

in a letter. 'She was unconscious for four hours yesterday – and then she suddenly asked for tea. She cannot possibly recover and she suffers a lot of pain at times, so we hope it will soon be over; but she has wonderful vitality for any age – let alone 93.'

Mrs Potter died in December 1932. The favourite maid, Lucissa, later said that she always thought that Beatrix had more sympathy for her Herdwicks than for her mother. 'When Mrs Potter was dying . . . she said "I just can't waste my time here." She even started to take things out of the sitting-room before she had died. There was no love lost between mother and daughter.' It is easy to criticise from the outside, and Lucissa (who was favoured enough to be left fifty pounds in Mrs Potter's will) only saw the last years of the relationship, not all the decades

that had gone before. She didn't know either about the two marriages Mrs Potter had tried to stop. She and her daughter were both strong-willed ladies, selfish about their own concerns.

Beatrix could strike strangers as being abrupt and uncaring, especially as she grew older and more formidable. Tom Storey, for all his loyalty, said she could be 'funny', sometimes ignoring him or saying very little, and she was once very unsympathetic when his wife was ill. There is a story told in Grasmere about a couple, her tenant farmers, to whom she gave notice after the death of their son. She maintained they could no longer farm without him. When Beatrix arrived at the farm some time later, the farmer's wife bolted the door and wouldn't let her in.

ABOVE: *Honister, from the quarries*
LEFT: *Buttermere and Haystacks*

There are far more stories about her kindness, however: to her tenants, to the village of Sawrey and to Hawkshead, and to organisations she helped or even set up, such as the Hawkshead and District Nursing Association. Her gruff exterior seems to have been more off-putting than the person underneath. Old people who lived in Sawrey and Hawkshead as children remember her as rather frightening, and recount how they were warned by their mothers not to cross or upset her. She would quickly complain if any local children trespassed on her property or interfered with her animals. One man from Hawkshead remembers passing Beatrix's home every day when he was delivering milk as a boy in Sawrey. He used to catch sight of her coming out of the pig sty at Hill Top, at the same time every morning. 'Poor thing,' he used to think, 'she has to sleep with the pigs.'

Did she really like children? There are enough moans in her later letters to indicate they annoyed her. She had none herself and, like the Blessed Wainwright, appeared as she got older to much prefer animals to children. Her letters show a growing dislike of what she considered the spoiled and modern brats of the day. (Another cry that will always be with us.) But for many years she did give a very popular children's Christmas party in the village.

In her old age, it's fair to say she became eccentric, rather than uncaring. Her habit of wearing strange, scruffy clothes might have begun partly as affectation, Beatrix throwing herself into the rural part, but the habit stuck. The clothes grew scruffier and weirder as she got older, which alarmed the local children. Some might keep out of Mrs Heelis's way when she walked down to the village, but they all rushed to gape when her mother called, an eccentric in a rather different way. They loved to see old Mrs Potter arrive with all her grandeur. In the early days she came in a coach and pair, with a coachman and flunkey to help her out. They all giggled if Beatrix got in to go for a ride, sitting there in a tatty apron beside her mother in all her finery. Mrs Potter was known behind her back as Queen Victoria. Perhaps Beatrix's jumble-sale clothes were a reaction against her mother's life-long, ladylike, South Kensington obsessions.

LEFT: Storm clouds over Coniston
BELOW: Ullswater

What the children and chance acquaintances would never know was that she was self aware; behind that often alarming and rude exterior she could be funny at her own expense. Throughout her life, her letters and *Journal* show a dry wit, the sort of humour that Jane Austen perfected, a caustic dryness that can be easily missed, as in this account of the death of her pet mouse in 1886, when she was twenty. 'On October 18 occurred the death of Poor Miss Mouse, otherwise Xarifa. I was very much distressed, because she had been so sensible about taking medicine that I thought she would get through, but the asthma got over her one night, and she laid herself in my hand and died. Poor little thing, I thought at one time she would last as long as myself. . . . I wonder if another dormouse had so many acquaintances, Mr Bright, Mr J. Millais and Mr Leigh Smith had admired and stroked her, amongst others.'

You get this dry wit in her books, matter-of-fact and slightly mocking. When electricity arrived in Sawrey in the 1930s, she refused to have it in the house, but agreed to have it in the 'shippons', the covered barns for cattle. 'The cows may like it,' so she told Tom Storey. Not very funny, not really worth repeating, but very BP.

In 1935, she became friendly with a local artist called Delmar Banner, newly arrived in the Lake District. (He did that 'farm wife' colour portrait of her, now in the National Portrait Gallery, which you see on post cards.) He has given an account of the first time he and his wife met her, which shows a nicely affectionate image of Beatrix in her old age. 'We knocked at the door of Castle Cottage one October afternoon. It opened and we beheld one of her own characters; yet better than any: short, plump, solid, with apple-red cheeks; she looked up at us with keen blue eyes and a smile. On her head was a kind of tea-cosy, and she was dressed in lots of wool. "Cum in," she said in a snug voice, and led the way. In the room into which we followed her bent and venerable figure there were bookshelves, a mahogany dining table, silver candlesticks and a cheerful fire. . . . We noticed . . . her husband's slippers warming on the fender and (for her age) a rather naughty quantity of silver chocolate paper on a little table.' That tea-cosy hat she wore was noted by many people. Even funnier, so people said, was when she was out in the fields in hot weather and wore a rhubarb leaf on her head.

In the spring of 1940 she surprisingly agreed to see a New Zealand fan, even though he had revealed in his letter that he was also a journalist. 'I hate publicity,' so she replied to him, 'and I have contrived to survive to be an old woman without it, except in the homely atmosphere of Agricultural Shows.' But he was eventually allowed to come for tea and she showed him the original artwork for many of her books. Peering over a picture of Jemima Puddle-duck trying to fly, she laughed loudly. 'That is what I used to look like to Sawrey people. I rushed about, quacking industriously!' I see her more as Mrs Tiggy-winkle, especially in her old age, bustling around in an old apron, still being ever so busy, with her hair pins sticking wrong end out.

RIGHT: Ullswater

ABOVE: The wild side of Lakeland: Wastwater

ABOVE: Woods by the side of Coniston

She kept up a correspondence with her New Zealand friend during the first few years of the war, describing the state of the country: 'If things get worse, I think I'll bury some tins of biscuits in the woods!' She was very ill at the beginning of the war, going to the Women's Hospital in Liverpool for a hysterectomy in 1939, from which she did not expect to survive. She wrote to her next-door neighbours, asking them to look after Willie and urge him to marry again. She did recover however, and also survived very severe flu during the bad winter of 1942.

In the autumn of 1943 Beatrix caught bronchitis and was confined to the house. 'I have plenty to do indoors and the little dogs [her two Pekinese] are great company – most efficient footwarmers.'

She died on the evening of 22 December 1943. Willie was by her side. He requested no flowers, no letters, no mourning, and arranged for her body to be cremated.

In Beatrix's will, she left most of her personal possessions to Willie for his lifetime. (He died a year and a half later.) But she also remembered the nephew of Norman Warne, her fiancé who died, leaving him her shares in the company, and after Willie's death, the royalties from her books. The National Trust became the main beneficiary, receiving four thousand acres of Lakeland property, which included fifteen farms and numerous cottages. She instructed that the rooms at Hill Top should be kept as she left them and the house not be let to a tenant. The sheep stock on her fell farms should remain pure Herdwick. The National Trust have obeyed her instructions to the letter: Herdwicks on her Hill Top and Troutbeck farms still have an 'H' branded on their side to this day. So her smit lives on, as do her animals and farms, her books and characters, part of Lakeland life for ever.

Beatrix Potter has become a name known with affection throughout most of the so-called civilised world. Her book sales in the year she died were 219,000 copies. In 1987 they reached seven million. The United States now comprises her biggest public, followed by Britain, but not far behind in sales comes Japan. Her very essence, however, lives on in the soil of the Lake District. Three days after her death, on Christmas Day 1943, Tom Storey was having his Christmas dinner when Mr Heelis walked into the house. He remembered the scene exactly when I talked to him that time in 1979, as he tended a bonfire in the field beside Hill Top.

'"Here's the ashes," so he said to me. "You'll know what to do with them." I'd promised her I'd scatter them. Nobody else was to know, not even her

ABOVE: *The hills above Hill Top. Is this where Beatrix Potter's ashes were scattered?*
LEFT: *Windermere*

husband. We'd discussed it several times. I talked to her about it the night before she died.

'So I got up from my dinner and went off and scattered them, in the place she had chosen. I've never told anybody where the place is. She wasn't daft. She knew folks would go and look at the place if they knew. I was sorry when she died. She was a good woman. I intend to tell my son the place before I die, so there will always be someone who knows . . .'

It must be somewhere around Hill Top. Perhaps on that little hill which she had first measured with pride, all those years earlier.

ABOVE: *Beatrix Potter with a young friend, Alison Hart, and one of her little Pekes, in 1942, the year before she died.*